Sadie Rose
AND THE DANGEROUS SEARCH

Other Crossway Books by Hilda Stahl

The Sadie Rose Adventure Series

Sadie Rose and the Daring Escape
Sadie Rose and the Cottonwood Creek Orphan
Sadie Rose and the Outlaw Rustlers
Sadie Rose and the Double Secret
Sadie Rose and the Mad Fortune Hunters
Sadie Rose and the Phantom Warrior
Sadie Rose and the Champion Sharpshooter
Sadie Rose and the Secret Romance
Sadie Rose and the Impossible Birthday Wish

The Growing Up Adventure Series

Sendi Lee Mason and the Milk Carton Kids
Sendi Lee Mason and the Stray Striped Cat
Sendi Lee Mason and the Big Mistake
Sendi Lee Mason and the Great Crusade

Kayla O'Brian Adventures

Kayla O'Brian and the Dangerous Journey
Kayla O'Brian: Trouble at Bitter Creek Ranch
Kayla O'Brian and the Runaway Orphans

Daisy Punkin Series

Meet Daisy Punkin
The Bratty Brother

Best Friends Series

#1: Chelsea and the Outrageous Phone Bill
#2: Big Trouble for Roxie
#3: Kathy's Baby-sitting Hassle
#4: Hannah and the Special 4th of July
#5: Roxie and the Red Rose Mystery
#6: Kathy's New Brother
#7: A Made-over Chelsea
#8: No Friends for Hannah
#9: Tough Choices for Roxie
#10: Chelsea's Special Touch
Special Edition #1: The Secret Tunnel Mystery

A SADIE ROSE ADVENTURE

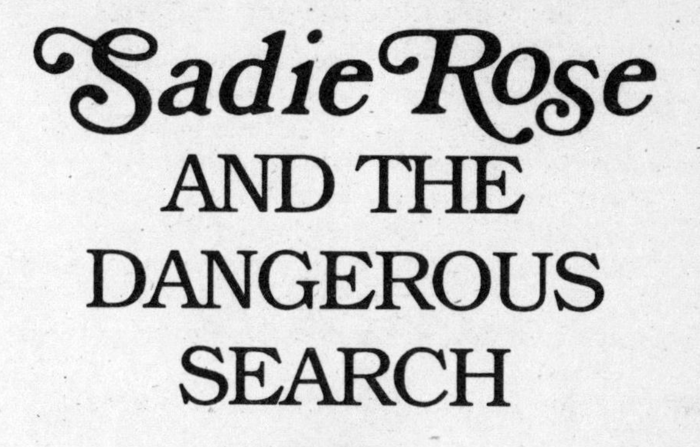

Sadie Rose AND THE DANGEROUS SEARCH

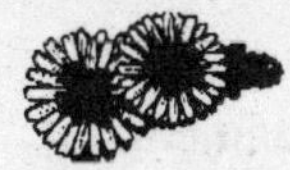

Hilda Stahl

CROSSWAY BOOKS • WHEATON, ILLINOIS
A DIVISION OF GOOD NEWS PUBLISHERS

Sadie Rose and the Dangerous Search.

Published by Crossway Books, a division of Good News Publishers, 1300 Crescent Street, Wheaton, Illinois 60187.

Cover illustration: Robert Spellman

First printing, 1993

Printed in the United States of America

Library of Congress Cataloging-in-Publication Data

Stahl, Hilda.

Sadie Rose and the dangerous search / Hilda Stahl.

p. cm. — (A Sadie Rose adventure)

Summary: Thirteen-year-old Sadie Rose and a runaway woman from Boston depend on their faith when they lose their way in a snow storm and are taken captive by rustlers on the Nebraska frontier.

[1. Frontier and pioneer life—Nebraska—Fiction. 2. Christian life—Fiction.] I. Title. II. Series: Stahl, Hilda. Sadie Rose adventure.

PZ7.S78244Sacc 1993 [Fic]—dc20 92-37204

ISBN 0-89107-715-4

01 00 99 98 97 96 95 94

15 14 13 12 11 10 9 8 7 6 5 4 3 2

Sadie Rose
AND THE DANGEROUS SEARCH

Contents

1

The Snowy Ride

Shivering, Sadie York hunched into her gray wool coat and clung to the saddle horn and the reins. A wool scarf held her hat tightly on her head, covered her ears, and wrapped around her neck. She'd pulled it up over her mouth and nose, and now it was frozen there. With a low nicker Apple carefully picked her way after Caleb's big bay and Riley's sorrel mare. They were looking for Circle Y cattle that had drifted away with the storm. Just then a blast of icy Nebraska wind whipped snow across the prairie and around Sadie, almost blinding her. The blizzard had stopped early this morning, but the wind continued to blow the snow as if it were trying to rearrange it against the rolling hills and wide valleys.

Sadie wanted to shout to Caleb, "Let me go back. It's too cold." But she kept the words locked inside herself. She knew Caleb and Riley needed help taking the cattle back. She was thirteen years old and way too old to complain about hard work. Just this once she wished she could, but Caleb was her daddy, and she had to obey him. She shivered and ducked her head against another blast of biting, stinging snow. How she'd like to be snug in the sod house finishing the valentines she'd been making with Helen, Web, and Opal! Momma had given them tiny pieces of lace and scraps of material to glue to the colored paper Flynn Greer, their teacher, had handed out Monday at the close of school. Next Friday was Valentine's Day, and there would be a big party for the students, families, and friends.

Caleb turned in the saddle and shouted, "You okay, Sadie Rose?"

She barely nodded and urged Apple to a faster walk. It would be terrible to get separated from Caleb and Riley. Sadie shivered at the frightening thought of being all alone in the vast Nebraska prairie with snow blowing so hard it was impossible to tell east from west or north from south. Late yesterday the blizzard had come howling down from Dakota Territory, and the cattle had bunched against the fence, knocked it down, and then wandered off into open range. Riley had discovered it before breakfast this morning when he'd gone to check the cattle. About thirty head were gone. Losing the cattle meant losing the frame house Caleb planned to build Momma in the spring. Momma hated living in the sod house.

"I want a wood floor, not a hard-packed dirt floor—and real walls made of wood, not chunks of sod cut from the prairie," Momma had said when she was at her wit's end. "I want room enough for all of us. Seven people need more than two rooms!"

Sadie watched Caleb ride toward another hill. She knew he really wanted the frame house for

Momma. He'd married Momma after Pa had died in the blizzard, and he'd brought all of them to his ranch at the edge of the sandhills. But he hadn't told them he lived in a tiny sod house. Momma had almost cried when she'd first seen it, but she kept her tears back, as usual, and made things do. She was good at making things do.

Sadie wrinkled her nose. She knew how to make things do too. She looked down at the overalls that Riley had once worn. Under the overalls were long johns that Riley had worn before he grew as big as a man. Now he was seventeen and longing to be eighteen so he could live on the land Caleb had bought for him. Sadie was stuck with his overalls and his long johns until Web grew into them. After that, they'd be Helen's. Opal had never had to wear Riley's overalls or long underwear even though she was fifteen. She helped in the house and with the chores but never helped round up cattle, train horses, or do the branding like Sadie did, so she had no need for them.

Sadie's toes tingled with cold inside her hightop shoes. How she wanted to huddle up to the stove and get warm clear to the bone! Would she ever be warm again? They'd been riding an hour already. If they found the cattle now, it would be an hour's ride back to the Circle Y. Could she make it? She barely nodded. She had to. "Help me, Jesus," she whispered. "And help us find the cattle soon."

Suddenly Caleb and Riley stopped their horses. They turned to wait for Sadie. They had their scarves pulled over their noses. Caleb looked warm in his big sheepskin coat. Riley's coat was warm, but he looked as cold as Sadie felt.

"I caught sight of them a minute ago," Caleb said in his soft Texas drawl as he pointed ahead.

Sadie couldn't see a thing through the swirling

snow, but she trusted Caleb. If he said he'd seen the cattle, he'd seen them. He was a man of his word.

"I'll circle around to the left of them. Riley and Sadie, you circle to the right. Ride real slow so you don't spook 'em. They're headin' away from us, so swing wide around 'em, and together we'll turn them back."

Riley nodded. He glanced at Sadie, then led the way. He knew to go around a hill instead of over it. Many of the hills were perfect on one side but completely or partially blown away on the other. Such a situation was dangerous. In the spring Helen had fallen into a blowout and couldn't climb out because the sides were too sandy. She'd climb partway up, then slide right back down to the bottom of the hole. Sadie had rescued her by tying her apron string to her bonnet string. She'd dropped it over the edge to Helen, then held on tight while Helen climbed out. Now the blowouts were full of snow—snow deep enough to trap a horse.

Sadie kept Apple close to Riley's sorrel. Just then the wind died down, and the snow settled to the ground. The sun tried to peek through the gray sky. Sadie could see the cattle, and she sighed in relief. By midafternoon they'd have the cattle back in the pasture and be inside the warm, snug sod house. She'd finish the valentine she was making for Levi. She grinned behind her scarf. Would he like getting it from her, or would it embarrass him? Maybe he'd give her one too. For the past several weeks he'd paid a lot of attention to her. If Opal and El Hepford hadn't been in love, would Levi have eyes only for Opal the way he used to?

Sadie frowned. She wouldn't think about that! She wanted to believe Levi was learning to love her. Her pulse tingled.

Riley looked over his shoulder and pulled his scarf off his mouth. "Sadie, swing further out and come up in front of the herd."

She nodded. It was safe to ride away from Riley now that the wind had stopped and she could see around her. She nudged Apple and rode a wider circle than Riley. She rounded a small knoll, and for a minute Riley and the cattle were out of sight. She urged Apple to go faster. Suddenly a rabbit leaped out in front of Apple. Sadie jerked on the reins, and Apple reared, almost sending Sadie flying. But she clung to the saddle horn and stuck in place like a burr. Apple settled down, and Sadie relaxed. She knew she shouldn't have jerked on the reins. Apple was a trained cow pony, and the horse couldn't be spooked by a rabbit or anything else.

The wind started to blow again, sending gusts of snow flying against and around Sadie. She peered into the white swirl but couldn't see anything. But it really didn't matter. She would continue on the way she was headed. Soon she'd be in front of the cattle and meet up with Riley and Caleb. She rode in silence, waiting for the wind to die down again, but it continued to send the snow swirling through the air. Her very bones felt frozen. Just how long would it take to reach the front of the herd?

A great silence surrounded her. Slowly the realization hit her that somehow she'd missed the herd, and she'd missed Caleb and Riley too! She was all alone on the prairie without any sense of direction. Trembling, she reined in Apple. A wild cry of fear rose inside her, but she bit it back. She wouldn't scream! She'd stay in one place until the wind died down again, and then she'd find Caleb and Riley. But what if she stayed in one place and froze solid? Her muscles tightened in alarm.

Apple lifted her head and whinnied.

Sadie laughed in relief. Apparently Apple sensed or heard someone nearby. "Take me to him, Apple." With her knees Sadie nudged Apple, loosening the reins to give her her head.

Apple stepped forward carefully. Sadie clung to the saddle horn, trying to see ahead through the white curtain. She draped the reins lightly over the saddle horn to keep from dropping them from her numb fingers.

Just then she heard a voice. "Riley?" she whispered. She didn't want to call out and sound like a frightened child, or to do anything that might spook the cattle either.

She rode closer and made out the dark blur of someone huddled under a blanket at the base of a hill. Sadie frowned. It wasn't Riley. He'd never dismount and let his horse run away. Sadie peered through the swirling snow, hesitated, then rode right up to the person. "Are you lost?" Sadie called loudly enough to be heard over the wind.

The person jumped up, and the blanket fell to the snowy ground. Sadie jerked on Apple's reins. The horse reared high. Too numb to hold on, Sadie slid right off the saddle and over Apple's rump and landed in a pile of snow. Apple raced away, the reins hooked over the saddle horn. If the reins had dangled down, Apple would've stayed put because Caleb had taught her to do that.

Her heart hammering with fear, Sadie struggled to her feet and stared at the stranger.

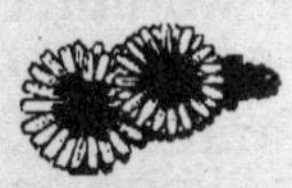

2 The Stranger

Sadie took a step toward the stranger, then stopped. It was a woman! She was bundled in a heavy leather coat like hunters wore and heavy hightop boots. Bright red strands of hair dangled from under her wide-brimmed hat. Her blue eyes looked wide and frightened in her freckled face. She was probably in her twenties. "Who . . . who are you?" Sadie asked hesitantly.

The woman darted a frightened look around, then stared hard at Sadie. "Who are you?"

"Sadie Merrill." Sadie started to correct herself. Caleb York had adopted her, so she was really Sadie York, but in her agitation her old name had slipped out.

"Are you alone?" the woman asked sharply.

Sadie shook her head. Why was the woman so frightened? "My daddy and my brother are here too."

The woman held the blanket to her as she looked around frantically. "Where?"

Sadie waved in the direction where she thought the cattle were. "I got separated from them because of the blowing snow. What about you?"

The woman nodded. "The same."

"We'll wait here. Someone will find us."

"But we can't wait here! We have to find your family."

Sadie shook her head. "My daddy told me to stay put if I ever got lost."

"We could look for him!"

"Wandering around on the prairie is dangerous. What if we walked the wrong way? We could end up deep in the sandhills where nobody lives."

Trembling, the woman glanced around again. The heavy mittens she wore made her hands look large. "Are we near your home?"

"An hour from it."

"Are we near anyone's place?"

"Jewel Comstock and the bachelors live along Cottonwood Creek to the north of us." Sadie chuckled. "I forgot. Sven Johnson got a mail-order bride. And Carl White is plannin' on one comin' too."

The color drained from the woman's face.

"Is something wrong?"

The woman's voice rose in panic. "We'll freeze to death out here!"

Sadie gasped at the terrible thought, then shook her head. "God is with us. He'll watch over us."

The woman gripped Sadie's arms. "Do you know God?"

Sadie nodded.

"So do I! But nobody else does. I thought I was

the only one." Tears filled the woman's eyes. "I'd given up! But God sent you to me! Are you an angel?"

Sadie giggled and shook her head. "Do I look like one?"

Finally the woman smiled, making her look almost as young as Opal. "What'll we do now?" She held out her blanket. "Please, share this with me to keep warm." She darted another look around. "I hope your family finds you soon before . . ." Her voice died away, and she trembled.

"Is something wrong?"

The woman shrugged. "Only that I'm lost and afraid of freezing to death."

Sadie knew it was more than that, but she didn't pry. She looked all around but could see only swirling snow. Would Apple find Caleb or return to the Circle Y? If she returned home, Momma would be upset and worried. With a sigh Sadie huddled under the blanket with the woman. The blanket smelled like sweat and blood. Sadie's stomach turned, but the blanket was too warm to refuse.

"Do you have a gun?" the woman asked sharply.

Sadie shook her head. "My brother and my daddy do."

"I don't have one either." The woman sounded agitated.

"If we had a gun, I could signal my dad and brother."

The woman nodded. She huddled deeper into the blanket. "I'm Cloris Rupert. I'm sorry, but I forgot your name."

"Sadie."

"Sadie. Call me Cloris."

Sadie nodded.

"You're probably wondering how I came to be here."

"You don't have to tell me if you don't want to." But Sadie was really very curious and wanted to know.

Just then the wind died down again, and the snow settled to the ground. Sadie looked all around. She saw a light gray sky and snow-covered hills and valleys, but no cattle and no sign of Caleb or Riley. Which direction was the Circle Y? Were they close to another ranch? She turned to Cloris. "I'm going to climb that tall hill and see if I can see anyone or hills I can recognize."

Cloris caught Sadie's arm. "You can't!"

Sadie pulled carefully away, frightened by the wild look in Cloris's eyes and the terrified sound of her voice. "Why not?"

"*They* might see you!"

Sadie frowned. "Who are *they*?"

Cloris ducked her head. "I . . . I can't tell you."

Sadie moved away from Cloris. What was going on? Were they in some kind of danger that she knew nothing about? The silence stretched on and on. "Are you running away?" Sadie finally asked.

Cloris barely nodded. "I just had to!"

Sadie knew Momma wouldn't want her to ask, but she had to know. "Who are you runnin' from, and why?"

Cloris shuddered. "It's a long story."

Sadie stepped closer to the hill. "Will you tell me?"

Cloris pulled off her big hat. Her hair looked flame-bright against the white hill. She awkwardly pushed her hair back and settled her hat back on her head. "They made me come with them. I came from Massachusetts, then went to Dakota Territory.

I was satisfied to stay there, but *they* said they needed a good cook on their hunt. I refused to come, but they brought me by force." She swallowed hard. "They came down for beef and antelope for the gold-fields."

Sadie gasped. "Beef? *Our* beef?"

Cloris bit her lower lip. "I don't know. Whatever they can find. And they don't care what brand the cows are carrying."

Sadie's heart raced. She couldn't let them steal Circle Y cattle! "I have to see where we are! I have to go to the top of that hill and look!"

Cloris's eyes filled with tears, and she hopelessly shook her head. "Don't. Oh, please, please don't! If they see you, they'll get us. They won't let you go."

"I have to take that chance."

"Then I'll go with you! I can't be alone any longer!"

Sadie nodded and waited while Cloris rolled up the blanket, tied it into a bedroll, and draped it over her shoulder. "Let's go." Sadie walked toward the hill, thankful the wind hadn't come up again. If it stayed quiet until she could look around, she could probably get her bearings. She'd take Cloris home with her, and she could stay in the small sod house with Adabelle Hepford, Judge Loggia's future wife.

At the top of the hill Sadie looked all around at the vast whiteness. Some of the hills had bare spots with dried grass showing. Finally she caught sight of a mass of brown. "Look! Cattle! They have to be ours!"

Cloris narrowed her eyes and looked. "I hope it's not the hunters," she said in a weak voice.

"We'll head that way, but be careful until we know it's Riley and Daddy. Let's go!" Sadie ran down the hill the way she'd gone up. Silently she thanked God for leading them in the right direction.

Sadie hurried in the direction of the cattle. It was hard to know how far away they were. She glanced at Cloris and saw the strained look on her face. "We'll be careful," Sadie said with a smile.

Cloris shrugged.

A rabbit jumped around a knoll, then sped away, leaving a trail behind it.

As she walked, Sadie's toes tingled with cold and felt wet. Clumps of snow hung at the bottoms of her overalls. The cold air hurt her forehead. Her legs ached, but she trudged on.

"How much further?" Cloris asked, shivering.

"I don't know. I'll climb that hill and see." Sadie stopped at the base of a hill. "Wait here. I'll be careful."

Hugging her blanket, Cloris sank to a spot clear of snow. "I'm very tired."

"Me too," Sadie whispered as she started up the hill. When she was almost to the top, she dropped to all fours and crawled the rest of the way. Her knees got wet and cold, making her shiver.

At the top she eased herself up and looked for the cattle. She could see them in a wide valley trying to find grass under the snow. No human was in sight. Her heart sank. She'd desperately wanted Caleb and Riley to be with the cattle. She strained to see the brand the cattle wore. She couldn't. They'd have to get closer.

A few minutes later she stood beside Cloris and told her about the cattle. "We have to look at them. If they belong to the Circle Y, we'll stay with them until my brother and daddy come for them."

Cloris nodded slightly. "The hunters have a wagon. If we see one, we'll hide."

Sadie agreed as she forced back a shiver. Cloris was scaring her. Were the hunters as bad as Cloris thought?

Just then a sound drifted through the silence of the sandhills. Sadie held her breath and listened. Her heart plunged to her icy feet. It was the sound of jangling harness and the creak of a wagon.

Cloris turned as white as the snow around them. "It's them," she hissed. "I know it!"

Sadie trembled, but then a calmness settled over her. "We'll listen and watch. If it comes closer, we'll duck out of sight behind a hill." She'd played hide and seek with Web, Helen, Opal, and Riley many times, hiding behind low hills or in the deep prairie grass. She looked down at her feet, then in the direction they'd come from. Their tracks stood out boldly in the snow. If the wind didn't come up and blow away their tracks, anyone could find them by simply following their footprints.

As the sound of the wagon grew closer, fear pricked Sadie's skin. How could they hide from the people in the wagon?

Cloris began whimpering as she stared toward the sound. She turned to Sadie. "We can't just stay here! Let's go," she whispered.

Sadie nodded. Didn't Cloris know they were almost sure to be followed and caught?

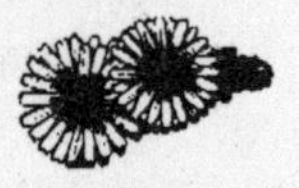

Hiding Out

Sadie ran after Cloris, grabbed the smelly wool blanket, and rubbed out footprints, then trailed the blanket behind them as they walked. It worked like a big broom. Anyone who knew how to track would spot what she'd done, but a greenhorn looking for footprints wouldn't. Hopefully the hunters weren't trained trackers. Shivers ran up and down Sadie's spine as they walked away from the sound of the wagon but toward the cattle. Where were Riley and Caleb? What if they'd missed each other and were wandering around trying to find each other and her? Sadie forced back a moan. It was too awful to think they might be wandering the prairie, or worse yet, had been shot by the hunters!

Cloris stopped and caught Sadie's arm. "Listen!"

Sadie lifted her head and pushed her scarf off

her ears so she could hear better. Men's voices drifted across the stillness. Trembling, Sadie moved closer to Cloris and pointed ahead. "Let's duck around that little hill."

"We must not let them catch us!"

"Don't worry. We won't." Sadie wished she was as sure as she sounded. She hurried toward the little hill, dragging the blanket carefully after them. The blanket was light enough to erase footprints, but not heavy enough to leave a deep path in the snow. Oh, why didn't Riley and Caleb come!

Her pulse racing, Cloris balled her hands into tight fists inside her mittens. Should she trust Sadie enough to tell her the whole truth? She stopped behind the hill with Sadie and waited. Cloris listened but couldn't hear anything except their breathing. She wouldn't tell Sadie more than she'd already told her. There was no need to.

Sadie felt Cloris's tension and wanted to ask her more questions but didn't. Cloris was a grown-up. It wouldn't be proper to pry into her life.

After several minutes Sadie motioned to Cloris and they walked on, heading toward another low hill. The refuge of the next hill beckoned her, but she also knew the risk they were taking. Two people walking across a valley would be very easy to see.

Sadie's legs ached with cold as she walked on and on. Finally she stopped again. She heard a cow moo and smelled fresh manure, and her heart leaped. The cattle were around the hill from them! She smiled at Cloris.

"We have to be careful," Cloris whispered.

"I know," Sadie answered in a low voice. She crept along the base of the hill, stopping to listen every few minutes. Finally she stood in plain view of the cattle. They'd found a valley with very little snow and were chomping off the dry grass. Steam rose from piles of manure. Sadie eased along between the hill and the cattle until she could read the brand. Circle Y! The cattle were theirs! Now all she and Cloris had to do was wait for Caleb and Riley.

Sadie smiled at Cloris, but she looked too scared to smile back. Was she afraid the men were hidden on the other side of the cattle? Sadie studied the area but couldn't see anything except the animals' shaggy winter hair, curved horns with pointed tips, and the cattle's breath hanging in the air.

Cautiously Sadie walked around until she found a sandy blowout that wasn't full of snow. She opened the blanket for Cloris, and they sat with their backs against the sand and the blanket around them. Sadie's stomach growled. She pulled off her glove and reached into her coat pocket for the biscuits wrapped in a white cloth napkin Momma had given her that morning. She gave one to Cloris and bit into the other. It was dry, but it took the edge off her hunger. Her canteen of water and her bedroll were on Apple. Sadie swallowed and tried to work up spit to keep her mouth from feeling too dry.

The wind came up and blew swirls of snow across the valley, but not into the air the way it had before. The cattle turned their backs to the wind and kept grazing. The silence stretched on and on. Sadie longed to hear the music the Hepfords made with all their instruments or to hear Caleb strum his guitar and sing. He could sing well enough, but nobody could compare with the big redheaded mountain man, Judge Loggia. In her mind she could hear the hymns he sang each Sunday, as well as the foot-stomping songs he'd written as praise to God.

"I can't stand the silence any longer," Cloris whispered sharply.

"Me neither."

"Tell me about your family."

Sadie tugged the scarf away from her face. The smell of wet wool turned her stomach. "We used to live in Douglas County in a frame house, but we moved after my Pa died. Momma and Caleb York fell in love and got married." Sadie blushed just thinking about how open Caleb was in showing his affection for Momma. Pa hadn't been like that at all. "Caleb moved us into a sod house on his ranch." Sadie narrowed her eyes and could see in her mind's eye what she'd seen that day. "I had wanted to stay back in Douglas County, so I wasn't happy about the move. But in town I'd saved a pup from being beaten, so I was occupied with taking care of him. Tanner is his name. He's big now and stands guard over all of us and our place." Sadie listened for sounds around her, then continued, "Riley's seventeen, and he's the oldest. He hated being a farmer, but he loves ranch work. Opal is next. She can t wait to get married and have her own home and kids. She and Ellis Hepford are talkin' about marryin' even though she's only fifteen."

Cloris laughed softly and shook her head. She would've gladly married at fifteen, but no one had spoken for her. "Where do you come in, Sadie?"

"After Opal. I'm thirteen, but I look younger because I'm small for my age. Momma says I take after Grandma." Sadie wrinkled her nose. "I don't like being short and thin! Web is almost as big as me, and he's only ten! Then there's the baby of the family—Helen. She's nine, and she hates being the baby. She's a little spoiled." Sadie sighed. "Helen and Web and Opal are at home right now, probably making valentines."

"Are you making a special valentine for a boy?"

Sadie grinned and blushed. "I started one." She didn't want to tell Cloris about Levi, so she said, "Tell me what you did back in Massachusetts."

Cloris hesitated, then decided it didn't matter if Sadie knew. "I was a servant."

"A servant?" Sadie had never met a servant before. She'd read about rich folks who had other people wait on them, but she couldn't imagine what one would look or be like. A hired hand could be called a servant, she supposed. "Who did you work for?"

"A rich man and woman." Cloris cleared her throat. "My aunt and her husband actually."

Sadie frowned. It would be like Gerda being Momma's servant. That was laughable! Gerda hadn't done anything for anybody until she'd married Gabe Hepford a few months ago.

"Aunt Prescott wouldn't allow me to go to work for pay at another home. She said it would humiliate her." Anger rose in Cloris even as she talked. "She wanted me to work for her because she didn't have to pay me! I worked for her from the time I was eleven years old!"

"What happened to your folks?"

"They got killed when their buggy tipped over." Cloris could remember it as if it had just happened. "Aunt Prescott took over the way she liked doing. She was my momma's sister." Cloris studied the blanket wrapped around her but wasn't seeing it. Instead, she saw Aunt Prescott. "Momma never got on well with Aunt Prescott. Actually, nobody did."

"Why couldn't you go somewhere else to live?"

Cloris bit her lip and felt the icy cold on her teeth and lips. She'd never talked about her past with anyone, but for some reason it seemed all right to tell Sadie. Cloris cleared her throat, then began.

Cloris Rupert's Story

With scalding tears in her eyes, Cloris tried to hide behind Aunt Prescott at the funeral, but her aunt pushed her forward. Aunt Prescott wore a heavy black dress, proper for mourning, that took up space for two people. She was a tall, well-built woman with a square chin and a mass of dark brown hair piled just right for the black hat she wore. She smelled like roses, a smell that didn't suit her at all.

"You want people to think you don't honor your own parents, Cloris?" Aunt Prescott hissed. "You're eleven years old—not an infant—so act like it!"

Tears slipped down Cloris's cheeks as she slowly walked to the caskets sitting end to end against the wall of the parlour. Her new black dress made her itch and felt heavy on her slight frame. Her head hurt from her long hair being braided too tight.

Aunt Prescott thought flame-red hair wasn't suitable for a funeral or for any occasion. But right now Cloris couldn't think about her hair or her freckles or her clothes. She didn't want to look at Mother and Father without life in them. She didn't want to see their bodies.

"They look so natural," Aunt Prescott said as if it had been her own doing.

Cloris turned her head to look, but after a quick glimpse she shut her eyes. When Grandfather had died last year Mother had said, "His body is here to bury in a grave, but Grandfather himself went to live in Heaven. Remember that, my precious Cloris, and the passing won't hurt as much."

Cloris thought about that now. The passing hurt, but she knew Mother and Father were in Heaven because they'd accepted Jesus as their Savior. Maybe after greeting Jesus, they were talking to Grandfather. Cloris smiled.

Aunt Prescott jabbed Cloris in the back and hissed in her ear, "Wipe that smile off your face! Do you want people to think you have no heart?"

Cloris ducked her head and tried to ease past Uncle Daniel. He was taller than Aunt Prescott and weighed close to three hundred pounds. He couldn't be moved unless he wanted to be. His black suit hung loose the way he'd demanded the tailor sew it. He scowled at Cloris, and she stayed wedged in between them, her eyes on the tips of her black shoes.

An eternity later she sat on the edge of the huge bed in the bedroom across from cousin Marlene, who was eight years old and spoiled rotten.

Cloris wanted to run home, but Aunt Prescott had said the place now belonged to strangers because Father hadn't paid his bills before he died.

Uncle Daniel had sold the house the same afternoon Father and Mother died, then had paid off the creditors and kept the rest of the money to defer the cost of raising a poor relative. Cloris had heard Uncle Daniel tell his neighbor all that this morning before the funeral. He'd kept her pony, Curly, for Marlene.

A tear trickled down Cloris's freckled cheek. How could she live without Mother and Father? They'd loved her. Aunt Prescott certainly didn't. Cloris didn't know why.

The bedroom door opened, and Bernice, the upstairs maid, walked in. A small white cap was perched on her wavy brown hair. She smiled. "Don't let your auntie see the tears or she'll be very cross with you. Dry your face, and let me help you get ready for dinner."

"I'm not hungry."

"No matter. You must eat with Miss Marlene in the nursery. Mrs. Vines said so." Bernice quickly unbraided Cloris's hair and rebraided it loosely so it wouldn't hurt. "You're to change from that dress to this one." Bernice held up a green dress Cloris had almost outgrown. "Miss Marlene likes green. She said she wouldn't eat if you wore black." Bernice chuckled. "And we all know that what she says is law around here."

Cloris thankfully took off her black dress and slipped on the green one. She felt lighter and a little more herself.

Bernice poured water into a basin and watched as Cloris washed her hands and face. "My mother knows of a way to rid yourself of those freckles if you're interested."

"No, thank you." Cloris swallowed a lump in her throat. "Father is . . . *was* . . . partial to freckles."

"Don't let Mrs. Vines hear that or she'll see you don't keep them."

Cloris gripped Bernice's hand. "I hope you stay here forever! I can bear it if you're here."

Bernice pulled her hand away. "Don't go on like that. You know what your aunt would do to me if she thought you cared for me."

Cloris nodded. "I'm sorry. I won't let her know."

"Nor Miss Marlene. She's a real tattletale if ever there was one. But don't breathe a word that I said so."

"I won't! I give you my word of honor."

Bernice smiled. "I know you always keep your word. I've watched you."

Cloris lifted her chin and felt a little better. Maybe she could endure living here after all.

A few minutes later Cloris sat across the table from Marlene. She wore a pink lacy dress with a white pinafore. A big pink ribbon held back her long brown hair. Her face was screwed up into a pout.

Bernice quietly served the dinner of baked fish, green beans, and small potatoes.

Marlene pushed her plate across the table to Cloris. "You eat my fish so Momma will think I did."

Cloris shook her head. "I can't."

"You better or I'll scream."

"I'm not hungry."

Marlene opened her mouth to scream, but Bernice stepped to her side.

"Miss Cloris is too sad today. She isn't trying to make you feel badly."

"Then *you* eat my fish!"

Cloris folded her hands in her lap and watched Bernice struggle with what to say. Marlene was a very spoiled girl!

"If you don't eat my fish, I'll tell Momma you stole her brooch."

Bernice's eyes flashed, but she kept her voice even. "You have the brooch, Miss Marlene. I didn't take it. I don't steal."

"I know that." Marlene tossed her head. "But Momma will believe me. We both know that."

Bernice picked up the plate and quickly ate the fish. She set the plate in place and handed Marlene a clean fork. "The fish was delicious."

Cloris hid a smile.

Marlene scowled at Bernice. "You're only saying that to make me wish I'd eaten it."

Cloris took a small bite of her fish. It *was* delicious, but it stuck in her throat. "She's right, Marlene. It is good. It's too bad you let Bernice eat it. You'd have liked it."

Marlene grabbed Cloris's plate, slid the fish onto hers, and quickly ate it.

Cloris picked at her food and managed to eat a few beans and two tiny potatoes. She drank half her cold milk, then dabbed her mouth with her white linen napkin.

After Bernice cleared off the table, Marlene said, "I want to play jackstones. But you have to give me more chances because I'm only eight and you're eleven."

Cloris wanted to snap at Marlene, but she quietly gave in. It wasn't worth the fight.

As the days passed, Cloris found it was never worth the fight. Marlene wanted her own way about everything, and she liked to win the games they played together.

One night when Cloris was fifteen Bernice slipped into her room. "Miss Marlene told her mother a lie about you today. I came to warn you."

Cloris jumped out of bed and pulled her robe on. "What did she tell her?"

"That you stole a kiss from the gardener's son."

Cloris gasped, her hand at her throat. "But that's not true! I was talking to Blue, but I never let him kiss me! Marlene is jealous because she knows Blue doesn't like her at all." Though a full twelve years old, Marlene was obnoxious and unattractive.

"I know it's not true, but I had to tell you. I don't know what kind of punishment Mrs. Vines will give you." Bernice patted Cloris's arm. "I must go before they catch me here."

Cloris hugged Bernice tightly. "Thank you. Again! How would I have survived without you?"

"You're a sweet girl. Keep trusting Jesus."

"I will." Cloris watched Bernice slip back out the door, then crept back into the high bed. She lay with her eyes wide open for a long time. Moonlight shone across her floor from the tall windows. The smell of candle wax hung in the air. "Jesus, help me tolerate living here until I'm eighteen and can leave."

The next morning Aunt Prescott called Cloris to the morning room just after breakfast. Cloris stood in the doorway as Aunt Prescott sat at a small round table near the windows and poured herself another cup of coffee in the fine china cup she favored. The cup and saucer were covered with delicate blue and pink and yellow flowers that looked much like the flowers in bloom just outside the windows. Aunt Prescott wore a lightweight pearl-gray dress with a white lace collar and cuffs. She set her cup down and frowned at Cloris.

"Sit down, Cloris."

Cloris sank to the chair across from Aunt Prescott. Sunlight brightened the small room. The smell of baking bread drifted from the kitchen.

Aunt Prescott folded her hands in her lap and looked down her nose at Cloris. "I've heard the most distressing report."

Cloris lifted a red brow. "Oh?" Her stomach knotted, but she kept her face calm. She'd learned to do that down through the years.

"I know you're fifteen and a young lady ready to attract young men. But it is beneath you to flirt with the hired help. I've learned that you kissed Blue." Fire shot from Aunt Prescott's eyes. "I won't have it, Cloris Rupert!"

Cloris felt her temper rise, but she forced it back under control. "Aunt Prescott, I would never kiss Blue or any young man."

"Are you calling me a liar?"

"No. But you were told an untruth."

Aunt Prescott lifted her chin. "I have decided it's time to take action."

Cloris trembled at the tone of Aunt Prescott's voice and the look on her face. "Do you plan to send me to finishing school like you intend to do with Marlene?"

"How forward! Cloris, you are a poor relative, not the daughter of the house, even though you were given schooling as if you were. All those years of piano lessons and voice lessons! What a waste of money!" A muscle jumped in Aunt Prescott's cheek. "You will never go to finishing school, but you will go through the school of hard knocks."

Cloris sucked in her breath. "Do you plan to put me out?"

"Not at all. You will become part of the staff in this house. You will wait on Marlene, and you will take care of the needs of others on the second floor."

Cloris stiffened. Had she heard right? Was she to become a servant?

"Bernice will train you. At the end of two weeks we'll let her go, and you'll take her place . . . and her room. Naturally, you won't receive any pay. After all, you are a relative who has lived off us for years."

Cloris stared in unbelief. She'd be Marlene's maid? How could Aunt Prescott do this? How could her aunt send her to the tiny room on the third floor? It was too much! "Why are you doing this?" she whispered hoarsely. "I didn't kiss Blue! We talked together. That's all!"

Aunt Prescott's face looked like one of the stone statues in the garden. "I won't listen to your lies or your arguments. You are dismissed!"

Cloris slowly stood, then ran from the room, her face white and her heart heavy. Was this what Aunt Prescott had planned all these years?

In her bedroom Cloris flung herself across the bed and sobbed. She heard the door close, and she jumped up, rubbing at her tears. Looking grief-stricken, Bernice walked over to her. In a rush of words Cloris told Bernice everything.

"I'm so sorry, Cloris. If I could stop her, I would, but I can't."

"I don't want you to lose your job!"

Bernice glanced at the closed door, then whispered, "I had planned to tell you tomorrow . . . I'm going to be married in two weeks, so I would've quit anyway."

"Married! To Stan?"

Bernice giggled and nodded. "He finally got the courage to ask me. We'll live on the farm, in the house provided for him."

"I'm happy for you! But I'll never get to see you!"

"We'll work it out. I'll come into town to trade, and we'll meet somewhere."

Cloris agreed. Bernice was her only friend. She would not lose her!

Later in the nursery that was now the schoolroom, Marlene pointed to Cloris and laughed. "You're going to be my maid. And you'll stop taking classes with me. Now I'll be the smartest!"

"Because you'll be the only student." Cloris faced Marlene squarely. "Think of this, cousin—you'll also be the dumbest!"

Marlene's cheeks turned bright red, and she doubled her fists at her sides. "You don't deserve to live here! How I've hated you all these years!"

Cloris walked out with Marlene screaming behind her.

Two weeks later Cloris sat on the straightback chair beside the narrow cot that would be her bed until she turned eighteen. "Once I am eighteen, I'll leave this house to never return! It's only three more years. I can do this for three years."

She burst into tears, then covered her face with icy hands and sobbed.

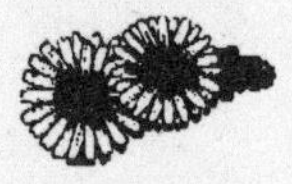

5 The Story Continues

Cloris set her cup of tea down and smiled across the kitchen table at Bernice. The past three years Cloris had visited Bernice two hours a week—all that Aunt Prescott would allow. The tiny house was like home to her and Bernice like an older sister. Outdoors icy February wind blew around the barns and the trees, but inside the coal stove kept it warm. Cloris smoothed her gray wool dress over her knees. "Today is my last day to work for Aunt Prescott. Thank God the time is finally over!"

Bernice checked her baby boy in the wooden cradle beside her, then leaned forward, her eyes sparkling. "Now that it's finally here, I have a surprise for you."

"You do? What?" It was probably a box of candy for her valentine birthday.

"I talked to Mrs. Aberdeen about you. She said

the minute you're finished with the job you have now, you're welcome to work for her as governess to her three children."

"Governess! Oh, Bernice, is it really true?"

Bernice laughed softly and nodded. "I've told her about your good education, and she was very impressed. She'll pay you two dollars a week plus room and board."

"So much! I'll finally have money of my own!" Cloris's eyes filled with tears. "You've been a good friend to me all these years. Thank you!"

"It'll be fun having you here at the farm all the time instead of a once-a-week visit." Bernice glanced out the window toward the main house, then grinned impishly at Cloris. "I think Gray likes you. It would be wonderful if you married him. He plans on going into partnership with his brother on the farm. It's a good living."

Cloris flushed, and her heart skipped a beat. Secretly she liked Gray and could easily fall in love with him. Maybe now they'd have a chance. "I'll be here early in the morning with all of my things."

"I'll send Stan in with the wagon to fetch you. It's too blustery for you to walk so far."

"That would be very nice indeed. Oh, but I will be glad to leave that terrible place! I never want to step foot in Aunt Prescott's home again! Nor see Marlene. She has been worse than usual."

Just then the baby cried, and Bernice excused herself to nurse him and change his diaper.

Cloris sipped her tea as she stared dreamily out the window. Soon she'd live at the farm in the main house and get paid for the work she'd do. It was almost too good to be true. It would be strange living in the country instead of in Boston, but she'd get used to it.

At six o'clock, back in town, Cloris laughed under her breath as she hurried to Marlene's room with the dinner tray decorated with red valentine hearts trimmed with white lace. The smell of fish drifted out from the covered plate. Marlene had complained of yet another headache, but Cloris knew Marlene couldn't tolerate having dinner with the family when old Mr. Nash was a guest. He had been a business associate of Uncle Daniel and continued to be important to him. Mr. Nash drooled when he ate, and he talked with his mouth full. He always told the same stories about his days aboard ship when he was in the fishing business. He stayed at the docks most of the day and smelled like raw fish. Cloris liked to listen to him. On the days when she went to the fish market at the docks she'd talk to him. Marlene hated that, though she enjoyed watching the ships come and go.

Cloris slowed her steps, dreading seeing Marlene. "This is the last tray I'll carry for her," Cloris whispered with a giggle. Today was her eighteenth birthday. In the morning she'd walk out of Aunt Prescott Vines's big, impressive house never to return! Cloris stopped in the hall to steady the excited beat of her heart. For the first time ever she'd receive payment for her services. She'd be able to attend church regularly instead of when Aunt Prescott allowed her to go. Her life would finally be her own.

She pushed the bedroom door open and slipped inside. Marlene stood at the window, looking toward the Boston harbor. Her brown hair hung down her back and fanned across the blue wool dress she wore. At fifteen, on the outside she was a real beauty, but being hateful on the inside made her appear ugly.

"Here's your dinner, Miss Marlene." Cloris had learned long ago not to choke each time she addressed her cousin so formally. Aunt Prescott had insisted on the title. Cloris set the tray on the small round table at the left of the huge bed. The flowered bedspread matched the drapes and the covering on an armchair and a chaise. A fire crackled in the brick fireplace.

Marlene turned with a scowl. "I suppose you visited Bernice today."

Cloris nodded.

"You certainly look pleased with yourself! I suppose you'd rather live on that dreary farm than here." Her blue eyes narrowed, Marlene stood with her hands on her narrow waist. She wanted to be able to read Cloris's thoughts, but of course she couldn't.

Cloris shrugged. She would not let Marlene rile her, not today of all days!

Marlene was determined to see beneath the calm exterior Cloris always displayed. Was unleashed anger hidden there? "I'll ask Mother to keep you away from there."

Again Cloris shrugged. After today it wouldn't matter what Marlene did or said.

Marlene took a step forward, and her skirts swayed at her slender ankles. "Is there a man you're in love with at that farm?"

Cloris blushed, then frowned for having betrayed herself.

Laughing shrilly, Marlene ran to Cloris's side. "Did I meet him? Would *I* like him? Or is he a rough man without any manners or any schooling?"

"Eat your dinner, Miss Marlene. It's your favorite fish." Cloris pulled out the chair and motioned for Marlene to sit.

The demanding fifteen-year-old dropped to the seat and grabbed her napkin. "Why won't you ever talk to me about men? I'm not a child any longer! I don't care what Mother says—I'm going to meet men, and I will get married before I'm eighteen." Marlene's chin was set stubbornly. "Even if I have to run away to do it!"

Cloris lifted the cover off the food and stepped back. "But you'll want a large wedding with all the frills, and you won't get that if you run away."

"And you won't get it no matter what!" Marlene quickly ate her food, then wiped her mouth. "Can't you sit down and talk to me? Do you know how tired I am of being locked away in my room?"

Cloris covered the plate again and picked up the tray. "You could join your family for dessert."

Marlene burst into tears. Sometimes she was lonely beyond words. Today had been like that. She'd never had a friend to open her heart to like Cloris could do with Bernice. Life wasn't fair! No matter what she did, she wasn't happy. Just once she wanted to know what it felt like to be happy! "Please don't go, Cloris. Sit down and talk to me—cousin to cousin. Please." Marlene almost choked on the word *please*, but she was feeling desperate. The winter was stretching on far too long, and she wanted something . . . something she couldn't name.

Surprised, Cloris put the tray down and sat across from Marlene.

"Do you know I didn't get one invitation to a valentine party?"

"I'm sorry."

"I suppose you think I deserve that kind of treatment."

Cloris thought exactly so, but she didn't say so.

"I had a dress made special with hearts embroidered on it and red ribbons and lace." Marlene ran to her closet and reached inside for the dress. "Naturally it wouldn't look good on you with your hair and freckles, but it looks beautiful on me."

"I'm sure it does." Cloris looked at the dress and envied Marlene, then rejected the feeling. Someday she'd have all the dresses she wanted—red hair or not! "It's a beautiful dress. Why don't you put it on and wear it downstairs for your family and Mr. Nash?"

Marlene impatiently hung the dress back. She touched her other fine dresses. Tears burned her eyes. No matter what she wore, Turner Jefferson took no heed. She faced Cloris again. "Did you see Turner today?"

"No. Was he here?"

"Not as far as I know." Marlene sank to her chair and folded her hands in her lap. "Do you think he'll marry me when he graduates from the university?"

"I don't know."

"You do so! You don't think he will, do you? You think he's too intelligent and too nice for me!"

Cloris did think that but had never voiced it to anyone but Bernice. Marlene had fallen for Turner Jefferson the first time he'd come for dinner last year. Aunt Prescott had invited him because she wanted him to marry Marlene. He was from one of the old families of Boston, and his father was richer than Uncle Daniel. Finally Cloris said, "Turner is a fine man and would make a wonderful husband someday."

"Don't get any ideas of him wanting *you*!"

Cloris gasped. "I never would!"

"See that you don't. He'd never marry a poor relation of mine."

Cloris bit her lip to hold back a sharp retort.

Marlene took a deep, steadying breath. "Do you want to know the real reason I'm so upset?"

Cloris wanted to say, "You'll tell me anyway," but she simply said, "What made you so upset?"

Marlene looked toward her heavy door, then at Cloris. "I rose early this morning and peeked through the keyhole." Marlene shuddered. "And I saw only one object! One, not two as I should have. You know that means I won't get married this year!"

Cloris shook her head. "That's only a superstition."

"But it worked for Jane and even for that ugly old Leah!"

"Besides, you're fifteen. You don't want to marry until you're older."

"I want to marry now and get away from here! I'm tired of being smothered by Mother and ignored by Father!"

Cloris felt a stirring of sympathy for Marlene. "Why don't you travel abroad the way other girls do?"

"And spend the whole time being seasick? You know I love the water but can't travel on it."

"I'd forgotten."

"You, of course, never get seasick, do you?"

"No." Cloris glanced at the mantel clock. It was almost 9. She wanted to pack so she would be ready to leave just after first light in the morning.

Marlene saw Cloris look at the time, and anger surged through her. "You're bored! How dare you be bored talking to me?"

"I've had a long day, and I would like to return to my room."

Laughing, Marlene jumped up and pointed her finger at Cloris. "Did you know I'm the one who convinced Mother to move you to that tiny room on the third floor? I told her I wouldn't stay on the same wing with a servant. So she moved you."

Cloris slowly stood. "Why do you hate me, Marlene? What have I ever done to you?"

"You've treated me badly from the time I was a baby!"

"What? How can you say that?"

"Mother said you were copying your mother."

Cloris knotted her fists at her sides. "My mother was a wonderful person."

"She was not!" Marlene jabbed her finger at Cloris. "Your mother stole the man my mother loved!"

Cloris stared in shock at Marlene. Her mother and father had loved each other passionately. "That's not true!"

"Mother told me the whole story. She and Westland Rupert had their wedding day set, but then your mother stole him away."

Blood roared in Cloris's ears. She would not let Marlene mar the memory of her parents! "I won't listen to this. I'm going to my room."

"Not until I dismiss you!" Marlene caught Cloris by the arm. "You'll listen to every little detail."

Cloris jerked free and shook her head. "I won't! Not any longer."

An icy chill ran down Marlene's spine. "What do you mean by that?"

"I'm eighteen years old, and I'm leaving in the morning never to return!"

"Mother won't let you leave."

"She can't stop me!"

Marlene laughed softly. "Can't she?"

Cloris ran from the room and up the narrow flight of stairs to her tiny windowless room. A narrow bed stood against one wall, with a chair and a chest nearby. The room was cold, and Cloris was soon chilled to the bone. She closed the door with a snap and stood in the middle of the room, her chest rising and falling in agitation.

After a long time she sank to the edge of her bed and covered her face with her icy hands. "Heavenly Father, I need You now more than I've ever needed You before."

The next morning Cloris jumped up, lit her lamp, and finished packing the small case she'd brought to the house with her when she was eleven. She laughed right out loud. Today she'd walk away from this house and never return as long as she lived! Stan was probably already waiting outdoors for her.

She tied on her warm bonnet and buttoned her cape. Butterflies fluttered in her stomach. After today she'd never have to listen to Marlene or Aunt Prescott.

Cloris reached to open the door. The knob wouldn't turn. She tried again, but it still wouldn't turn. Was it stuck? She rattled it, then knocked sharply. Pain shot through her knuckle. She knocked again. One of the other servants would certainly hear her and help her. She waited, but no one came, not even Eunice, who slept just across the narrow hall.

"Eunice! Can you hear me? The knob is stuck! Help me! Eunice!"

"Cloris . . ."

She sagged in relief against the door. "Eunice, open the door for me, will you?"

"I can't, Cloris. Mrs. Vines locked you in and forbade any of us to let you out until she's ready to talk to you."

Cloris fell back, her eyes wide in alarm. "But why?"

"She says you plan to run away, and she won't allow you to. She said you belong here and must stay."

"No! No, Eunice! I just can't!" Cloris pressed her face tight against the door. "Please let me out. I'm going to live on the farm where Bernice lives. I have a position as a governess, and I start today."

"I'm sorry, Cloris, but I'll lose my position if I let you out. I can't afford to lose this job. You know that—what with my ma sick and Pa taking to drink again."

"Then take me to Aunt Prescott right now!"

"She's still abed. I'm to take you at 9."

Cloris trembled, and tears streamed down her cheeks. "Bernice's husband is waiting for me. Tell him what happened."

"I can do that, I guess."

Cloris heard Eunice walk away. Maybe Stan would break her out. Cloris shook her head. He wouldn't. He wasn't bold enough.

Slowly she walked to her bed and sank down on it. Maybe she should break the door down herself and walk out. She shook her head helplessly. It would be impossible for her to break down the heavy door. Besides, Aunt Prescott would stop her somehow, even if she had to have her arrested.

Slowly Cloris took off her warm bonnet and her cape and waited for nine o'clock.

When the time came, she followed Eunice downstairs to the morning room where Aunt Prescott was reading the newspaper. The aunt looked up with a scowl.

Cloris ran forward. "Why are you trying to keep me here? I'm eighteen years old and can be on my own!"

Aunt Prescott laughed drily. "No, Cloris. You

signed a paper stating that you'd stay with me until you turn thirty."

"What? I never!"

Aunt Prescott held a paper out to Cloris. "Read for yourself."

Her heart sinking, Cloris took the paper and read it. It did indeed say she'd stay in service to Prescott Vines until she turned thirty. It was signed in her own hand—or done by a very clever forger. "I didn't sign this—I know I didn't," she said in a dead voice.

"Oh, but you did. Remember the day I had you sign a couple of notes for me?"

Cloris nodded.

"I slipped this in with it, and you signed it."

"But without my knowledge! This is not legal!"

"My dear niece, it's your word against mine. Naturally, everyone would believe me." Aunt Prescott took the paper back and held it in her lap. "You may go now."

Cloris helplessly shook her head.

"And don't try to run away or I'll have you locked away in a mental home—the very one we've visited to try to improve conditions."

Cloris turned and walked away as though she was in a daze.

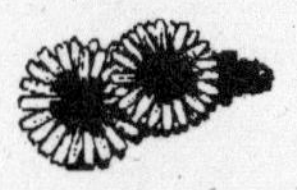

6 Love Letters

Cloris walked slowly across the yard while the wind tugged at her loosely piled hair. The white uniform swayed around her ankles. She'd left her blue apron in the kitchen while she took her stroll. Spring flowers bloomed in beds throughout the spacious lawn and along the brick drive. Horses nickered in the pen beside the barn. She looked longingly toward the tree-lined street. She could easily walk away from the house never to return. Her heart turned over. But if she did walk away and was caught, Aunt Prescott would without a doubt commit her as a patient to Westland Insane Asylum. Cloris sank to a wooden bench and looked unseeingly at the peonies. Two years ago she'd been late from trading at the docks, and Aunt Prescott had thought she'd run away. Aunt Prescott had gone after her, forced her into the buggy, and started for the asylum. It had taken Cloris several minutes to convince her she hadn't run away.

No, she couldn't run away. Not yet anyway. But she would devise a plan that would work. She'd find a way to leave the house, leave Boston, even leave Massachusetts so Aunt Prescott would never find her. She was twenty-two years old! Life was passing her by while she was a prisoner.

Just then Marlene stepped out onto the upstairs balcony and shouted, "Bring my mail to me, Cloris. And be quick about it!" Marlene had gone to Europe last year but had returned without any prospects of a beau.

Cloris hurried inside and picked up the mail from the front hall where Edward left it each day. Cloris leafed through the stack and pulled out two for Marlene. They were both from Nebraska from a man named Carl White. For the past three months Marlene had gotten letters from him, but she wouldn't offer any information about the man and why they were corresponding. Once Cloris had run across an open letter when she'd made Marlene's bed and had almost picked it up. The temptation had been great, but she'd resisted it.

She walked up the wide stairs to Marlene's room. Warm wind blew through Marlene's open window, bringing in the smell of the ocean. Marlene was stretched out on her lounge chair with a book in her hand. She dropped it to the carpet and took her two letters. Her heart skipped a beat, and she wanted to tear them open immediately but wouldn't do so with Cloris in the room.

Cloris straightened the curtains and picked up a comb and a glove off the floor. Marlene was not a tidy person, even though she always looked as if she were. Today she wore a light blue cotton dress with a row of tiny white buttons down the back. Her dark hair was piled neatly on her head and was held in place with bone hairpins. Cloris felt windswept and homely next to Marlene.

"Go away, Cloris!" Marlene jumped up, her cheeks rosy. "You can clean in here later!"

Forcing back a frown, Cloris walked out, then stood in the hallway. Who was Carl White? How had Marlene gotten acquainted with a man from Nebraska? It was very curious.

Slowly Cloris walked downstairs again. The smell of roses from the huge vase near the front door filled the foyer.

Aunt Prescott stood in the library door. "Be ready to leave for Westland immediately."

Cloris trembled. Why would Aunt Prescott go to the asylum now? It wasn't her day. "Is there a problem?"

"Yes! Do you think I'd go today to the asylum if there weren't?" Aunt Prescott turned away with a scowl.

Cloris ran upstairs to change. Aunt Prescott had told her to always wear her blue dress for the visits. Blue had a calming effect on the inmates.

A few minutes later Cloris drove the buggy down the brick street with Aunt Prescott wedged in beside her. Aunt Prescott's wide-skirted blue dress filled the seat, and the rose scent she wore blocked out even the smell of the ocean. The canvas top on the buggy shielded them from the warm sun. Cloris had been driving a buggy for years, but it had only been this year that Aunt Prescott had trusted her enough to drive when she was with her.

The streets were full of buggies, wagons, drays, and carts. Children ran along the side of the street, shouting. Women stood in groups, talking and laughing. Men tipped their hats to Aunt Prescott, and some smiled slyly at Cloris. She ignored them all.

Cloris stopped the buggy at the hitchrail outside the huge brick building. One wing of the building housed men, another women, and a third children. Cloris knew parents committed their children to the asylum if they disobeyed or were a bother to them even though nothing was wrong with them. Husbands often committed an erring wife—at times to be forgotten and other times for a week or so as a punishment. These persons were put in the same quarters as the worst—and most violent—inmates. Aunt Prescott was trying to put a stop to that practice. She'd told the board of the asylum that at least two doctors had to agree a patient was insane before committing him or her. And the doctors were to be men who couldn't be paid to agree with the one who wanted the person committed. Cloris gladly helped any way she could. She often took food and clothes to inmates while Aunt Prescott was in meetings. Marlene, on the other hand, refused to even drive down the street where the asylum was.

Cloris stepped from the buggy and tied the horses in place. She looked at the tall iron fence on one side of the asylum. Dirty faces peered through the grill work at her. Someone screamed; then several others did.

With a basket of freshly baked rolls on her arm, Cloris followed Aunt Prescott up the brick walk to the wide front doors. It was cool and quiet inside. However, Cloris knew only this part of the asylum was quiet. The rest was full of crying, shouting, screaming, talking humanity. The smell in the entrance and the offices was pleasant, but in the wings the stench was worse than any outhouse Cloris had ever been near. Often she had to hold her hanky over her mouth and nose to keep from vomiting. Aunt Prescott was also trying to get the place to meet a standard of cleanliness. So far she'd failed.

Aunt Prescott turned to Cloris. "I'll be in the meeting no more than one hour. Pass out the rolls, and meet me back here."

"I will." Cloris watched Aunt Prescott walk across the marble floor to the main office where the board always met.

Just then old Mr. Nash walked from the men's wing. His dark suit hung loosely on his slight frame. He staggered and caught himself against the paneled wall.

Cloris ran to him and took his arm. "Mr. Nash, let me help you. Sit down for a while."

"Cloris, it's you! Thank God!" He rubbed at the tears on his wrinkled cheeks. "I'm glad you came. I wouldn't put a dog in this place!"

"I know." Cloris eased him down onto a wooden bench, then sat beside him. "Why are you here?"

"To see Gus Bonney. I heard his boy had him locked up."

"I'm sorry. Did you find Mr. Bonney?"

Mr. Nash barely nodded. "It was terrible, Cloris! He didn't know me, and we worked together for years. He didn't even know me!" Mr. Nash wiped tears from his eyes. "He looked old. His hair was matted and full of fleas. His shirt was almost ripped off, and he had no shoes. I have to get him out of here, Cloris!"

"But maybe his mind is gone. Maybe he's dangerous."

"It couldn't happen in a month, could it?"

"I don't know." Cloris's stomach knotted at the thought of a sane man becoming insane from being in such a place. If Aunt Prescott locked her up here, would that happen to her? Abruptly she pushed the horrifying thought away. Aunt Prescott would never really commit her to Westland. She shivered and turned her attention back to Mr. Nash. "What do you plan to do?"

"Take him home with me . . . Clean him up . . . Feed him." Mr. Nash groaned. "He saved my life once, and I'm going to repay him."

"I'll help if I can." But what could *she* do? She wasn't very strong. And if she were caught, Aunt Prescott would be angry—angry enough to commit her. Cloris lifted her chin. None of that mattered. She'd help Mr. Nash bring his friend out of this awful scene. She had to. It would be worse than a nightmare to be in such a place.

"After I rest a bit, we'll walk to the men's quarters. While I get Gus, you distract the two men on guard."

"I can do that. They're always glad to see me because I share the food I bring for the inmates with them." Cloris wrinkled her nose. "I don't know how they can eat with the smell of this place all around them."

"I remember eating when fish was rotting around me. I don't know how I did it, but I did because I was too hungry not to."

"It would be hard for me." Cloris lifted the cloth from the basket and looked at the fresh rolls she'd brought. Ordinarily the aroma of freshly baked bread made her mouth water, but not this time.

Mr. Nash stood, squared his thin shoulders, and lifted his chin. "I'm ready if you are."

Cloris jumped up, the basket in her hand. "We'll have to hurry. Aunt Prescott wants me back here in less than an hour."

"We'll make it," Mr. Nash said grimly. "God is with us."

Cloris nodded as she hurried along beside the old man. The first guard, Jack, let them in without question. He'd seen Cloris there many times. She handed him a roll, and he thanked her and smiled a toothless grin.

Jabbering and sobbing men immediately swarmed around Cloris and Mr. Nash. Cloris handed them rolls to eat, while Mr. Nash searched for Gus. Abner, the second guard, hurried over to obtain his roll. Cloris asked him about his family and kept him talking while Mr. Nash quieted Gus enough to get him to walk toward the door with him.

"I have to go now, Abner. Give your family my regards."

"I'll do that, Miss Cloris. My missus thinks the work you do for these folks is real nice."

"Thank her for me." Cloris smiled and hurried over to Jack, who unlocked the door for her. She asked him about the dogs he raised. He told her about training a beagle and a setter, and meanwhile Mr. Nash and Gus slipped away to freedom.

Cloris's legs felt almost too weak to hold her as she gave Jack another roll and hurried out. She was just in time to see Mr. Nash slip out the front door and almost run to his buggy. He hid Gus under a lap robe and drove away.

An hour later Cloris returned home with Aunt Prescott. Cloris hurried to her room to change into her white uniform and apron. Mr. Nash was coming to dinner Friday night. She'd ask him then about Gus Bonney. Cloris smiled. What an adventure! *I wish I could tell someone about it, but I dare not!* she thought. Not even Bernice whom she saw at the market from time to time. Cloris wasn't allowed to visit her friend at the farm anymore.

Friday night Cloris found opportunity to speak to Mr. Nash in private when he was walking to his buggy. "Is Gus Bonney in good health?"

Mr. Nash laughed softly and patted Cloris on

the arm. "He is almost his old self. He still has nightmares about Westland, but he knows he's safe with me. Not even his son knows he's there. And we both mean to keep it that way."

"I won't breathe a word to anyone."

"I know I can trust you, Cloris. Gus said he wants to meet you someday."

"I'd like that." Cloris squeezed Mr. Nash's wrinkled hand. "Good night. God go with you."

"He always does. And with you too." Mr. Nash climbed in his buggy and drove away.

Slowly Cloris walked back to the house and slipped in through a side door the way she'd come out.

At the end of the summer Cloris once again carried mail to Marlene. This time there were three letters from Carl White.

Marlene grabbed the letters, then tossed them to the floor. "He bores me. If any more come, tear them up." She opened a carved wooden box and dumped the contents on the floor. "Take those letters too and destroy them! I'm done with a long-distance courtship! I'm going after Turner Jefferson."

Cloris's eyes widened. "But he's married!"

"I learned today that his wife died three months ago in childbirth. Isn't that wonderful? I'll go to Turner and make myself indispensable to him." Marlene laughed softly and patted her throat. "How can he turn down my love? He can't!"

Cloris trembled with anger as she gathered up the letters in her apron. She bit her tongue to keep back the stream of angry words. Would Marlene ever learn to love others? She was the most selfish person in the world!

Later, in her room, Cloris dumped all the letters on her bed. They scattered all the way across it, and two slid to the bare wood floor. She picked them up, and her heart jerked a strange little jerk. How could Marlene throw away love letters from Carl White as if they were no more important than the meatless claws of a lobster?

Cloris lit her lamp, then perched on her bed and picked up the letters one at a time. Some were thin and others thick. The handwriting was easy to read. She read the date posted on the worn-looking envelopes and put them in order. Suddenly she realized what she was planning to do—read the letters that weren't hers! She'd wanted to when she'd first delivered the letters to Marlene but couldn't bring herself to do so then. But now she would. But dare she? Her stomach fluttered. If Marlene learned she hadn't burned them but had kept and read them, she'd be angry enough to tell Aunt Prescott. That would surely mean punishment of some kind. The color drained from Cloris's face. What if the punishment was being locked in Westland Insane Asylum?

She dropped the letters as if they'd burned her. She stared at them, then looked at her closed door. No one would know she'd read them. When she finished, then she'd burn them.

She found the first one, opened it, and read it. When she finished, tears trickled down her cheeks. Marlene had answered an ad for a mail-order bride! She'd agreed to get to know Carl White through the mail to see if she'd be willing to go to Nebraska and marry him. He sounded lonely and kind. He loved the Lord and worked hard on his ranch. How could Marlene toss him so easily aside just to run after Turner Jefferson, a man who wouldn't give her a second thought?

Cloris picked up the letters that had arrived today. When she opened them, a train ticket fell from one and several dollars from the other. She gingerly touched the ticket and the money, her pulse leaping. She read the letters, and both flowed with words of love for Marlene. Both were full of excitement too because she'd agreed to marry him and to travel west to spend her life with him. He said he'd meet her at Jake's Crossing, Nebraska.

One by one Cloris read the letters. She learned to care for Carl White and his big white stallion Marengo. From her study of history she knew the horse had the same name as Napoleon Bonaparte's. She read about Sven Johnson and his mail-order bride, Kara. She read about the York family—Caleb and Bess and their children Riley, Opal, Sadie, Web, and Helen. She laughed over stories of the big-boned woman with the loud voice—Jewel Comstock—and the orphan girl Mary she'd taken in. She could hear the music of the Hepfords, and she enjoyed the love story between Adabelle Hepford and Judge Loggia. She felt as if she knew Joshua Cass, his son Levi, and Joshua's Pawnee wife, Lost Sand Cherry. The sod schoolhouse sounded strange but nice. She could see the good-looking teacher Flynn Greer and his sidekick Barr Eldred.

Long into the night Cloris read the letters, many of them several times. It was as if she'd stepped into a big family full of love.

"I won't burn the letters!" The whispered words startled her. "I'll hide them, and I'll use the ticket and the money to go there." The words clung to her dry lips. "*I'll* marry Carl White, and we'll grow in love."

A great weakness swept over her, and she pulled the letters to her, curled up on her bed, and fell asleep.

7 Escape

Cloris hurried toward Marlene's room with the breakfast tray in her hands. The pouch holding the train ticket and money was tucked securely in the hidden pocket in her petticoat where she'd carried it for the past week, ever since she'd read Carl White's letters. She had sewed the letters inside a pillow covering, then kept them inside a white pillow case on her bed. She figured that even if Marlene suspected the letters were in her room, she'd never find them. Now Cloris trembled and almost lost her grip on the tray.

Just minutes earlier, she'd hidden her suitcase and the pillow case with the letters under a bush at the side of the house. The gardener had worked in that area yesterday, so she knew he wouldn't be working on that side today. Tonight, before Eunice could lock her in her room, Cloris would sneak away from the house and hide in the train depot until early morning. This time she'd escape! She couldn't bear to think about the horrifying consequences if she didn't succeed. She'd lived with the fear of it too long. "Help me, Father God!" she whispered hoarsely.

She walked into Marlene's room and set the tray on the round table. Marlene was still in bed. Cloris opened the drapes and let in the sunshine. A pleasant breeze blew in and aired out the room. "Time to eat, Miss Marlene. You asked to be awakened early this morning."

Marlene yawned and stretched, then crept from bed. She pulled off her nightcap and shook her hair down around her shoulders. "I'm not very hungry. What did you bring me?"

"Tea and a muffin."

Marlene frowned. "That won't hold me until lunch! I want a scrambled egg and two pieces of bacon."

Cloris hurried to the door. "I'll bring them right up."

"No, wait! I need you to help me dress and do my hair." Marlene sat down and picked up the buttered muffin. "This will have to do."

"Yes, Miss Marlene."

"Something's going on with you, Cloris. What is it? Why are your eyes sparkling so?"

Cloris frantically searched her mind for something to say. Nothing—absolutely nothing—must keep her from escaping! "I'm wondering how it went with you and Turner Jefferson."

Marlene laughed softly. "I should've realized you'd be thinking of my romantic interests. *You* certainly don't have any."

Cloris pressed her hand to her skirt to feel the

pouch. Soon she'd meet Carl, and they would grow to love each other, then live happily ever after.

Marlene sipped her tea, then looked over the top of the china cup at Cloris. "Turner really is wonderful. He's coming for dinner tonight."

"How nice for you."

Marlene closed her eyes and sighed heavily. "I wish I knew what he wanted! He actually asked me to pray for him."

"He believes in prayer. But you must know that he's a fine Christian man."

"Don't start that again, Cloris. You know I'm not interested in religion."

Cloris gripped the back of the chair and leaned slightly forward. They'd had this same type of conversation many times. "It's not *religion*. It's having a personal relationship with God. He sent Jesus to be the Savior of the world."

"I know! Haven't I heard it every Christmas?" Marlene jumped up. "Fix my hair! And be quick about it!"

Cloris picked up the hairbrush and in a few minutes had Marlene's rich brown tresses piled becomingly on her head. She helped her with her undergarments, then patiently buttoned up her dress. Tomorrow morning someone else would do this for Marlene. Cloris immediately pushed that thought aside. She dare not think anything that would cause her to seem excited or nervous or Marlene would notice.

"Are you going to . . . that . . . that place today, Cloris?"

"What place?"

"I can't bear to say it aloud. You know very well what place I mean." Marlene lowered her voice to a whisper. "Westland Insane Asylum."

"Your mother and I are going." Cloris couldn't imagine why Marlene would ask. Marlene was never interested, nor would she listen to a word about the asylum from anyone.

Marlene studied her fingernails. "I told Turner I go there with Mother regularly."

"But surely he knows better!"

Marlene sagged in her chair. "He already asked me about the children's ward, and I had to quickly change the subject."

"Why did you tell him you go there?"

"He expects me to do good! He knows it's one of Mother's pet charities, and he seemed so impressed that she's been trying to make it a better place that I just had to say I went with her. Now I don't know what to do."

Cloris shrugged. "Tell him the truth."

"And lose him?"

Biting back a quick retort, Cloris folded Marlene's nightdress and tucked it under her pillow, then started making the bed. "Do you think he's interested in you?"

"Yes. Especially when I told him how I help others. It really is absurd." Marlene walked to the window and looked down at the mass of summer flowers that soon would be killed by frost. She turned and looked in distress at Cloris. "What am I to do?"

Cloris tugged the bedspread into place. "Go with your mother today to the asylum."

The color drained from Marlene's cheeks. "I can't," she whispered hoarsely. "You know I can't."

"But why?" Cloris turned to Marlene with a slight frown. "I could never understand why."

Marlene locked her fingers together. "Don't you know?"

Cloris shook her head. "Should I?" She'd always assumed it was because Marlene was so selfish.

Marlene's stomach tightened, and she couldn't speak for a while. She cleared her throat as she walked slowly toward Cloris. "My brother's in there."

Cloris gasped in horror. "No! How can that be?"

"I'm not supposed to know. Lyle's your age."

Cloris frowned in thought. Had she seen a man named Lyle on her visits? She knew many of the inmates by name, but she couldn't remember a Lyle. "So that's why your mother is so interested in the place."

"She blames you for what happened, you know."

"Me?" Cloris pointed to herself. "Me? I didn't even know about him!"

"I heard her talking about it with Father." Marlene shivered, then rubbed her hands up and down her arms. "Mother said your mother brought you for a visit when I was about a year old. You and Lyle were climbing trees, and you pushed Lyle out. He was never the same afterwards."

As Marlene talked, a picture flashed across Cloris's mind of two children playing in a tree. She saw the boy fall. Weakly she sank to a chair. "I remember," she whispered in agony. "But I didn't push him. He was showing off like he always liked to do. He started to fall, and I grabbed his arm. His shirt tore, and he fell."

"He was never the same after that. He couldn't speak, and he had fits. So they had him locked up at Westland." Marlene walked back and forth across the carpeted floor. "I was always afraid they'd do that to me if I did anything wrong."

"But they wouldn't," Cloris said absently.

"They might."

"They love you."

Marlene stood very still, her eyes downcast. "They loved Lyle too."

Cloris rubbed an unsteady hand across her forehead. As she thought more about it, she knew Aunt Prescott was capable of anything, even committing Marlene.

"I heard Mother say she'd have you locked up if you did anything wrong. I know she meant it."

"Me too." Cloris's voice broke, and she trembled.

"She could easily get angry at me and commit me." Marlene's face hardened. "I've pushed her to the limit at times just to get it over with."

"And she never committed you."

Marlene nodded slightly. "Maybe she wouldn't." She sat down across the table from Cloris. "Enough of that! I have to answer Turner's questions. How can I when I've never been there?"

"Do as I said. Go with your mother today. I'll stay home."

Marlene jumped up, and her eyes flashed with excitement. "I have it! You can tell me the answers to Turner's questions." Marlene clasped her hands at her heart. "Even better, you can come downstairs after dinner tonight. When Turner talks about the asylum, I'll have you tell him. He'll think I'm trying to make you feel like part of the conversation." Marlene nodded. "Yes! That's just what we'll do."

Cloris shook her head. "Don't ask me to do that!"

"I already have," Marlene said coldly. "Be downstairs just after dinner."

Cloris searched her mind for a way out. "I have nothing to wear."

"We're almost the same size. You can wear something of mine." Marlene opened her fancy closet and studied the contents. Finally she pulled out a pale yellow cotton dress with a flowered petticoat. "Try it on."

Cloris's nerves tightened as she took off her uniform, being careful to not let the hidden pouch show. She slipped on the petticoat and dress. It was a little short, but otherwise it fit. She glanced in the looking glass, then stared in shock at the pretty redhead looking back. She could pass as a lady of the house and not a servant.

Marlene scowled at Cloris. The dress had never looked that good on *her*. "You'll do, I suppose. Make sure you style your hair. Do you have shoes?"

"Only these." Cloris lifted her skirts to show her black hightops.

"Try on the yellow slippers that go with the dress. But be careful with them."

Cloris unbuttoned her shoes and slipped her feet into the soft slippers with a broad two-inch high heel. How slender her ankles looked! She kept her eyes down so Marlene couldn't see the pleased look. "They fit well enough for me to wear them."

"Then wear them," Marlene snapped. "But only for the time you're downstairs. When I dismiss you, you change out of my clothes immediately, then go to your room."

Cloris trembled. Going to the tiny room was sheer torture. She felt as if she were suffocating because she knew Eunice locked her in at Aunt Prescott's orders. Cloris took a deep, steadying breath. Tonight she'd be gone before Eunice could lock her in! To fool Eunice she'd arrange pillows under the cover to look as if she were in bed asleep. And after tomorrow she'd be free!

That evening Cloris walked carefully downstairs to the brightly lit front hall. The skirts swayed around her legs. The hip bustle felt strange. It was the first one she'd ever worn. She caught her reflection in the wide looking glass hanging between two lamps mounted on the wall and smiled. She'd pulled her flame-red hair back and looped it loosely at the nape of her neck. She'd pinned the pouch with the train ticket and money on the underside of the first petticoat. She couldn't take a chance on anyone searching her room and finding them.

The heels of her shoes clicked against the highly polished wooden floor as she walked to the open doorway of the front room. Laughter and the sound of voices drifted out. She hesitated, then walked in as inconspicuously as she could. Surely Marlene had remembered to tell Aunt Prescott about inviting her to join them.

Turner Jefferson was talking with Marlene near the bay window. Marlene looked on edge. Turner didn't seem to notice as he talked and smiled. His blond hair was combed back from his wide forehead. He had a medium build and was quite good looking. Across the room Aunt Prescott sat on the sofa talking to their overnight house guest, an older woman named Rachel Hightree. Uncle Daniel sat in a comfortable armchair and was deep in conversation with Mr. Nash, who was sitting in the matching chair.

Marlene hurried across the room to Cloris. "I'm so happy you could make it, Cloris dear!" Under her breath she said, "It's about time! I thought you'd be here long ago!"

"But Eunice only this minute called me down."

"Don't cause a scene." Marlene smiled brightly as she slipped her hand through Cloris's arm and led her over to Turner. "Turner, I'm sure you remember my cousin Cloris."

Smiling, he bowed slightly. "I certainly do! It's been a long time."

"I'm very pleased to see you again." Cloris smiled warmly. She'd always liked Turner. She wished she didn't have to help Marlene in winning his affection.

Marlene saw the flash of interest in Turner's eyes, and jealous anger rushed through her. "Let's sit down and talk, shall we? Turner, you'd just asked me about Westland." Marlene pinched Cloris's arm, then let it go. "Cloris, tell Turner what we've done for the children there."

Cloris talked about the clothes and food they'd gotten from the town merchants for the children. "A group of volunteers scrubbed the entire children's wing. And we had bars put on the windows so we could open them and let in fresh air."

"I'm glad to hear it. I'm impressed." Turner smiled into Cloris's eyes.

Marlene wanted to send Cloris to her room, but she couldn't until she was finished with her. The evening dragged on and on and on.

Cloris felt Marlene's tension increase until it felt as if she'd explode. Finally Cloris turned to Marlene. "I really should be going."

"Please, not yet," Turner said, reaching for Cloris's hand. "I'd like to invite you to dinner tomorrow."

Marlene jerked Cloris aside out of Turner's reach. "Cousin dear, didn't you tell me you're busy tomorrow?"

Cloris nodded. If only they knew! "I certainly am. I'm sorry, Mr. Jefferson. It was nice seeing you again. Excuse me please."

Turner took a step toward Cloris. "Could I take you home?"

"No!" Marlene snapped. "Cloris, I'll walk you to the door." Such anger raged inside Marlene that her vision became blurry. She stopped Cloris at the door. "You walk around to the side door and go right to my room, change, then get to your own room. If you don't, you'll be very sorry."

Cloris nodded. She'd never seen Marlene so angry. Would she make trouble for her? Cloris walked out into the warm summer evening. Moths flew around the lamps lit along the driveway. She heard the low pitch of a boat whistle and the close sound of a cat meowing. She ran lightly to the side door. Why couldn't she change now and keep running? She reached to open the door. The knob wouldn't turn. The door was locked! Who'd locked it? She'd told Eunice to make sure it stayed open. Maybe Edward locked it without Eunice knowing.

Cloris walked slowly through the flower garden, breathing in the scent of the beautiful flowers. In a minute she'd go to the kitchen door. She stopped at the bench among the flowers, but didn't sit down in case it was covered with dew and she ruined the dress. Oh, but it felt good to be free! She glanced toward the bush where she'd hidden her things, then laughed softly. Things would work out this time.

She heard Clarence bring a saddled horse as well as a horse and buggy to the front, then watched as Turner walked out with Marlene. He smiled and said good night. She stood on the step and watched him mount the saddled horse and ride away.

Cloris hurried toward Marlene. Before Cloris could speak Marlene spotted her.

"How dare you still be out here? Were you waiting to be alone with Turner?"

Cloris took a deep, steadying breath. "The door was locked and I couldn't get in."

"Don't lie to me! You could've gone to the kitchen door."

"I was going to."

"I don't believe you! I think you were going to run away. And that is exactly what I will tell Mother." Marlene narrowed her eyes and moved a step closer to Cloris. "You know what that means, don't you? Westland Insane Asylum."

Cloris's heart sank.

"But you have friends there, so it won't be so bad for you, will it?"

Trembling, Cloris held her hand out to Marlene. "Don't do this, Marlene. Please don't!"

"I'll tell her you stole my dress and shoes and were running away, but I caught you!"

Cloris could see Marlene was serious. Her anger and jealousy were so great that she'd send her to Westland without another thought. Cloris's blood ran cold.

Marlene turned to the door just as Mr. Nash told Daniel good night and walked out, his hat and cane in his hand.

"Evening, ladies," Mr. Nash said.

Marlene glared at him and stepped to the door. "Mother, I must see you now!"

Mr. Nash walked to his buggy and drove away.

Cloris ducked behind a bush, her heart racing and her head spinning with frightening thoughts. Could she get back inside before anything really dreadful happened? She started to move, then stopped as Marlene and Aunt Prescott rushed out.

"Mother, I know she ran away. And she stole my dress and shoes!"

"This time she will go to Westland!"

Cloris shivered so hard, she almost fell to her knees.

"And once she's there, she'll never get out! That's what she deserves after what she did to Lyle." Aunt Prescott turned toward the door. "I'll get my cape and go after her now. Tell Clarence to bring the buggy immediately."

Suddenly frightened, Marlene caught her mother's arm. "Are you sure you want to do this? I really didn't mean for her to go to that dreadful place."

"*I* meant for her to," Aunt Prescott said in a deadly voice.

Marlene moaned, her hand over her mouth.

Cloris waited until Aunt Prescott walked inside and Marlene went to call Clarence. Then she crept to the bushes where she'd hidden her things. Could she really run away? Silently she prayed for help. This time she had to escape! But could she? She picked up her things and dodged from tree to tree until she reached the street. Frantically she looked up and down the empty road. A dog barked from behind the brick house across the street. Moonlight filtered through the trees, lighting a path. "You are my strength, Lord," Cloris whispered. With her suitcase in one hand and the pillow case of letters in the other, she sped down the street in the direction Mr. Nash had gone. She had only minutes to get away. Dare she head for the train station? Would Aunt Prescott think to look there? She'd probably check the farm and Bernice first.

Up ahead Cloris saw a buggy stopped at the side of the street and a man checking a hoof on his horse. She hesitated, then ran faster. She recognized Mr. Nash as he climbed into his buggy again.

Could she ask for his help? Her heart thundered in her ears. He was a friend of the family. Would he take her back to Aunt Prescott? She had to take a chance.

"Mr. Nash . . ." she called softly.

Mr. Nash glanced back. "What's going on here?" he asked sharply.

Cloris leaned weakly against the buggy and looked up at Mr. Nash. "Please help me. They're going to send me to Westland because they're angry at me."

"That's ridiculous! The Vines would never do that."

"My aunt hates me. You know that . . . You've seen . . . Help me get away . . . Please!"

Mr. Nash pushed his top hat to the back of his head. "You're asking a lot, young lady."

"I know, but I'm desperate." Her voice broke. "Please . . . I helped you with your friend Gus Bonney."

"Yes, that's right, you did. I had forgotten. Get in."

Cloris climbed in. "If Aunt Prescott finds me, she said she'd have me locked up and I'd never get out."

"Not if I have anything to say about it!" Mr. Nash flicked the reins and drove away at a fast clip.

Cloris shivered. Was she really free?

"Where should I take you?"

"To the train depot."

"They'll look there." Mr. Nash was quiet for a while. "I'll take you to my house."

"Thank you! God bless you! My train leaves at 7 in the morning."

"I'll make sure you get there on time."

Tears of relief streamed down Cloris's cheeks.

She leaned back and silently thanked God for sending her help. She really was free—at last!

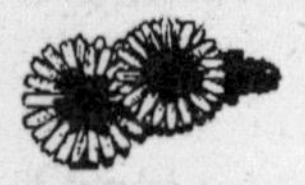

8
The Trip West

Her mouth dry, Cloris woke with a start. She felt the train jerk, then chug on. The hot rays of the sun shone through the open windows, turning the inside of the car as hot as the outside. The wind blew in cinders that burned holes in the seat or the passengers' clothing. Cloris jumped, then relaxed as the cinders fell short of the gray dress she'd decided to wear for traveling.

Even after three days of travel she was still jumpy. At the Boston station she'd wanted to peek out the window but hadn't dared in case Aunt Prescott was there. Now the train was far enough away that she didn't have to jump in fright each time it stopped, but she did anyway. Would it be that way all the way to Nebraska? Carl White had told her (not really her, but Marlene—yet it seemed like he'd been speaking directly to her) in his letters that it would take about a fortnight to get to Nebraska. There was no way Aunt Prescott could stop her now. She'd asked Mr. Nash to secretly return Marlene's dress and shoes, and he'd agreed. It wouldn't lessen Marlene's or her mother's anger, but it was only right for Cloris to see that the things were returned. She sighed heavily and tried to relax.

A man in his midthirties dropped down beside Cloris and smiled, flashing white teeth. He held a black bowler in his long-fingered hands. His dark hair was parted in the middle and combed straight down to his ears. "Afternoon. You looked lonely, so I thought why not join you and cheer you up."

"That's not necessary." Cloris smiled hesitantly. He was being very nice, but for some reason she felt a little nervous. The only strangers she'd been exposed to were those her aunt and uncle knew or the merchants with whom she'd dealt.

"My name's Jess Elsworth. I'm a traveling salesman." He grinned as he adjusted his tie. "I sell anything and everything, but I specialize in notions—perfumes, medicines, soaps, and much more. What about you? Who are you, and where are you heading?"

Cloris glanced around to see if she could call the conductor for help if necessary. He wasn't in sight. Stiffly she turned back to Jess Elsworth. "I'm going west."

"Ha ha! You're a funny one. We're all heading west. Me, I'm stopping off in Chicago." He leaned closer until his shoulder almost touched Cloris's. "You ever been to Chicago?"

"No." She pulled away at the smell of beer on his breath.

"You're more than welcome to fall in with me.

We could see the city together. I could teach you the trade."

"No, thank you."

Jess Elsworth leaned close again. "Me, I'm partial to redheads. Tell me about yourself—let's get acquainted."

Cloris looked helplessly around. A woman with a basket on her arm was walking down the narrow aisle. Cloris looked pleadingly at her.

She lifted her eyebrows questioningly, then stopped beside Cloris's seat and smiled at her. "I could sure use the company of another female."

"Yes, me too!" Cloris said in relief.

The woman glanced at Jess. "I heard the conductor asking about you."

"You did?"

"See for yourself." The woman shrugged, then stepped aside as Jess pushed himself up.

He smiled at Cloris. "Good talking to you."

Cloris inclined her head a fraction.

Jess walked away without a backward glance.

The woman smiled at Cloris. "Mind if I sit with you?"

"Not at all." Cloris smiled as the woman settled beside her. The woman was probably in her twenties with tangled brown hair, a thick waist, and wide hips. Her dark traveling dress was stained with perspiration and had holes burned in it from flying cinders. "Thank you for coming to my aid."

"Glad to help. We girls have to stick together."

"So it seems." Cloris liked the woman. "Thank you again. I didn't know how to get rid of him."

"I've been around all kinds and learned early on how to handle them all." She rested her arms on the top of the basket. "I'm Amanda Bodeen from New York. I got on yesterday."

"Cloris Rupert." She smiled. "From Boston."

"Boston, eh? I've never been out of New York."

"I've never been out of Massachusetts."

"Now we're both heading west to seek our fortunes. At least I am. I'm on my way to hunt for gold in Dakota Territory."

Cloris gasped as she stared in shock at Amanda.

"I know what you're thinking. How can a woman alone go prospecting for gold?" Amanda patted her ample bosom. "Well, this woman can and will! I heard enough about finding gold from all them folks I cooked for that I got gold fever as bad as the rest of 'em." Amanda shifted in her seat. "I'm tired of making a living cooking for a bunch of rich folk who want me to treat 'em like nobility." Amanda lifted her double chin. "I don't bow for no man! Or woman, for that matter. Where are you going?"

"To Nebraska."

"That's the state just south of Dakota Territory."

"Yes, I know. I checked the map."

"I've been planning on going to Dakota Territory for a year now. I got the map memorized." Amanda chuckled. "I could find my way on foot if need be. What's taking you west?"

Cloris hesitated. What harm would there be in telling? Besides, she could trust Amanda. "A man. We're getting married." That is, if she could convince Carl White to take her instead of Marlene who really didn't want him.

"Good for you. I had a couple of chances to get married, but I won't marry for anything but love." Amanda opened the basket. "I'm hungry. How about you?"

"Some. But I don't want to take your food."

"I packed plenty. I don't mind sharing with you."

Amanda pulled out a loaf of bread and sliced off a thick slice with a knife from the basket. She handed it to Cloris, then cut off a hunk of cheese. "I got apples too. The bread's not as good as it was yesterday, but it's not moldy or anything."

Cloris thankfully ate the bread and cheese, then an apple. The juice spurted onto her hand and chin, and she dabbed it with a napkin Amanda gave her. A man across the aisle was snoring loudly. A little girl slowly walked down the aisle and looked longingly at the apple. Her mother nudged her, and she walked on. Cloris wanted to call her back and share the apple with her, but she didn't.

When they finished eating, Amanda put the lid back on the basket and set it on the floor at her feet. "Next stop I'll fill the basket again so we don't run out. We could buy sandwiches from the conductor, but they're not very good."

"I know. I've had two." Cloris planned to spend Carl's money wisely so it would last all the way to Nebraska. The terrible sandwiches weren't a wise choice. She turned to face Amanda. "Did the conductor really want Jess Elsworth?"

Amanda chuckled. "I had to say something to get rid of him without upsetting him."

"I couldn't think of a thing to say."

"You'll get plenty of practice on this trip. It'll help if we stick together."

"I'd like that." Cloris folded her hands in her lap and relaxed for the first time since she'd run away. There was something about Amanda that reminded her of Bernice and made it easy for her to talk.

For the rest of the train trip Cloris spent all her waking time with Amanda. When they reached the roundhouse in Broken Arrow, Nebraska, where Cloris was to board a stage coach for the last part of her trip, they walked together into the hot sunshine. Cloris still felt the sway and jolt of the train. Her ears rang with the constant clatter and hiss.

Cloris looked down the dusty street toward the small buildings. Hot wind bent the three young trees that shaded part of the street. A few horses were tied at the hitch rail outside the saddle shop. A wagon stood outside the general store. Was this how Jake's Crossing looked? No, Carl had said the buildings there were made of sod. That was hard to imagine.

Suddenly Amanda started to cry. "I can't leave you."

Cloris led her to the side of the depot where they could talk privately. "Please don't cry, Amanda, or I will too." Tears burned Cloris's eyes, but she wouldn't let them fall.

"You're my first real friend, Cloris. How can I lose you now? Please change your mind and go with me to mine for gold." She'd pleaded the past three days for Cloris to do just that. "You don't know for sure Carl will even marry you."

Cloris shivered. She knew that what Amanda said was true, but she didn't like to think about it. She wanted everything to be as perfect in reality as in her daydreams. She squeezed Amanda's hand. "You could go with me. Find a husband. Or start a business or something."

"No! I'm sorry, but no. I'm going to the goldfields in Dakota Territory like I said." Amanda clutched Cloris's arms. "Please, please go with me! We'll ride north as far as the stage line will take us, then take a wagon to the goldfields. I already have a man who'll take us."

"I don't know . . ."

"Cloris, I heard there's gold right on top of the ground. You can pick it up and be rich overnight!"

Cloris's pulse leaped. Rich overnight! It sounded good, but. . . "I really can't."

"Yes, you can! You can go to Carl after you strike it rich! Go to him in the spring with your pockets lined with gold! Think of the good you could do for him and his ranch!"

The color drained from Cloris's face. "I don't know anything about finding gold!"

"Neither do I. We'll learn together." Amanda sighed heavily. "Cloris, I guess I'm being selfish, but I don't want to go alone. You and I are kindred spirits. We could help each other." Amanda bit her lower lip, and tears sparkled in her brown eyes. "I need your help, my friend. I don't think I can really go by myself to the goldfields."

"You're a smooth talker just like that notions salesman!"

"Does that mean you'll go with me?"

Cloris laughed softly. Just like that she changed her mind. She did want to offer Carl White more than herself. "Oh, all right, Amanda, I'll go with you. I would like to be rich too, and I would like to be with you a little longer."

"Oh, thank you!" Amanda hugged Cloris tightly, then released her and wiped her tears away.

Cloris straightened her hat, then eyed Amanda through narrowed eyes. "On one condition."

Amanda chuckled and waved. "Anything you say."

"You leave when I do and go with me to Jake's Crossing. We'll meet Carl White, and we'll find you a husband."

Amanda sucked in air. "I don't know. I planned to go back home in triumph so I could sit down and eat with the filthy rich—the very ones I cooked for."

Cloris laughed. "My plan is better, and you know it."

Amanda frowned in thought, then finally nodded. "All right, I agree. Let's get our stuff and head for Dakota Territory."

Cloris laughed breathlessly. She'd left Boston to marry Carl White, and now she was heading for gold country!

The next day they left the stagecoach, paid for baths, then hunted down Smokey Dunlop. He was a quiet, wrinkled, skinny man with an oversized mustache and a bald head that was covered by a wide-brimmed hat. He carried a whip and a rifle and knew how to use them. Two hours after that, they sat in the back of Smokey's wagon with the supplies he was taking into Dakota Territory. Amanda had contacted him months ago after she'd learned about him from a man in New York who'd been to the goldfields. No stagecoach line went that far north, and the only alternative was to hire Smokey or buy her own wagon and team. She didn't have enough money for the latter choice.

Cloris held her pillow with Carl's letters on her lap as the wagon swayed and bounced over the prairie. She looked at the sky that stretched on forever. "Have you ever seen such a sky?"

"I never knew it could be so big." Amanda leaned back and looked up at the blue sky and puffy white clouds. Wind blew her hair into more disorder. Her bonnet dangled down her back. "When there aren't any trees in the way, you really can see forever."

Cloris saw a herd of antelope and pointed them out to Amanda. This vast country was nothing like she'd pictured, even after reading Carl's letters. She and Amanda and Smokey were the only people as far as she could see. She hugged Carl's letters tighter.

At night the temperature dropped, and they huddled in their blankets close to the crackling fire. On the other side of the fire Smokey slept on the ground under a wool blanket as easily as if he were in a bed inside a house. So far he'd not said more than five words. Over the snap of the burning wood they heard coyotes, a wolf, and the screech of a cougar.

"God is with us," Cloris whispered. But it was hard to imagine Him being in the vast lonely wilderness. She knew He was, though, because He was with her always, no matter where she was. She thought about Carl White. Would he wonder where she was? She'd sent him a letter, saying to meet her in Jake's Crossing. He thought he was meeting Marlene, but he'd soon learn the truth and be glad for it. Wouldn't he?

Cloris moved, and Carl's letters crinkled. He was a man with a big heart. Surely it would be big enough to include her. Trembling, she closed her eyes.

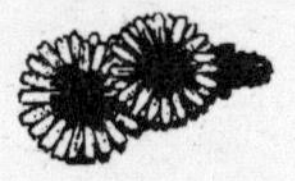

The Hunters

Holding her cloak tightly at her throat, Cloris walked up and down the muddy street and looked among the hodgepodge of wooden shacks in search for Amanda. January wind whipped through the camp, freezing the paths into ruts. "Where are you, Amanda?"

Cloris pushed back scalding tears. Life at the goldfields and in the gold camp had been nothing like they'd planned. Gold was not lying on top of the ground for anyone to find. Cold wind and icy temperatures combined with not having enough to eat had made life miserable. She hadn't been warm since they'd arrived. Neither of them could get the mining supplies they'd planned to buy because of the exorbitant cost of everything. Instead Amanda had opened a diner and once again was cooking for a living—this time in a wooden shack without glass in the windows. "It's better than starving to death," Amanda had said. In five months she'd lost so much weight that she was almost as thin as Cloris. With needle and thread Cloris had taken tucks in Amanda's clothes until they somewhat fit.

During those five months, Amanda had taught Cloris everything she knew about cooking and taking care of herself around strangers. They both worked from before daylight until long after dark. At night they fell into bed—actually, cold bedrolls on the floor of a tiny shack—and slept restlessly. Amanda hated not being able to search for gold. Cloris only wanted to get away, to go to Nebraska and to Carl White. Their tempers flared at the men who complained there wasn't enough food and even at each other over tiny everyday things. Just this morning they'd argued about who would make the coffee. Amanda had stalked off in a huff, and Cloris hadn't seen her since.

With a deep sigh Cloris stopped at the edge of camp and looked toward the prairie, then toward the ragged foothills. Finally she spotted Amanda standing on a low hill, her skirts flapping around her legs. Relieved, Cloris ran to her. Tears stood in her eyes. Cloris's heart turned over at the agony she saw on her friend's face.

"Amanda, I was so worried about you!"

Amanda rubbed at her eyes. "Cloris, what are we doing here? The only good that came out of this miserable trip is our becoming friends and me finally losing weight. But we're not getting rich, and we're always fighting, and I cry when anybody looks at me cross-eyed. What are we going to do?"

"Leave! Go to Carl White!"

Amanda sighed heavily. "Without gold?"

"Yes! We're miserable here, Amanda. Why

should we stay?" Cloris watched Amanda's thin face for any sign of surrender. Finally she saw it, and her heart leaped with excitement.

"All right!" Amanda acknowledged. "We'll go with the first wagon leaving here."

"We could hire our own wagon and driver."

"What with? We get paid mostly in promises."

Cloris bit her lip. "And I used the last of the money from Carl to buy beef in December. We'll have to start charging hard cash for food so we can get enough money to leave."

"And we'll have to get some meat to feed the miners. I saw some hunters ride in this morning. They look rough, but we should talk to them anyway." Amanda slipped her hand through Cloris's arm and headed back toward the dismal camp.

"Let's make a pact, Amanda."

"Okay."

"That we leave here before my birthday February 14."

Amanda squeezed Cloris's arm. "It's a deal."

Cloris laughed breathlessly. It seemed too good to be true, but they'd make it come true.

Several minutes later they sat together at a rough wooden table in their diner with Teeg, the boss of the hunters. He looked part Indian with high cheekbones, black eyes, and black hair. He straddled a chair and rested his arms across the back of it. His long coat dragged the floor near his scuffed boots. He smelled as if he'd just gutted and skinned a deer.

"How soon can you supply us with meat?" Amanda asked in her most businesslike manner. Nobody ever intimidated her, not even a hunter armed with a knife and a rifle who stunk up the whole camp.

"A week. No more 'n two." Teeg narrowed his eyes. "You pay half now and half when we get back."

Cloris held her breath as she watched Amanda at work.

Amanda shook her head. "You don't get any pay until we see the meat in your wagon. That's how we work. If you don't want the job, we'll hire somebody else."

Cloris sat very still. She knew no one else would go. The men were too caught up in finding gold to take the time to hunt for meat.

Teeg sprang to his feet and held out a dirt-encrusted hand to Amanda. "You got a deal."

Grinning, Amanda took the dirty hand as if it were lily-white. "See you in a week or two. The sooner the better since I promised Cloris here a big bash for her birthday."

Teeg eyed Cloris up and down, then walked out, his long coat swaying at his ankles.

The minute the door closed behind him, Cloris and Amanda jumped up, hugged, then laughed happily. Soon they'd have meat aplenty!

Later Cloris ran back to the shack to change into dry stockings before she set to work helping make dinner. She opened her pack of clothes and pulled out the stockings. They felt good on her icy feet. She laid the wet ones out to dry, then tied her work shoes. Just as she started to open the door, it swung in, and Teeg walked in with Ulrie, a big red-headed, red-bearded man who worked with him.

"Get out of here right now!" Cloris cried.

"You're comin' with us." Teeg thrust a paper at Cloris. "This is to leave for your friend."

Cloris read the childlike scrawl, and her blood turned to a million icicles pricking her insides. The note said, "We took the redhead to cook for us as pay for going after meat. She'll be in good shape when we get back or you don't have to pay us. Teeg."

"You can't be serious!" Cloris backed away from the men. But she could see by their faces that they were very serious. She knew she was too weak to fight them.

"Get your things and come on." Teeg motioned to the pack on the floor beside Cloris.

Helplessly she shook her head.

"You're going with or without your stuff," the big redhead said with a laugh that made his red beard shake. "Me and Teeg and Runt all agreed. You make even a peep and I'll hogtie you and gag you and toss you in the wagon like a side of beef."

With a moan Cloris picked up her clothes and her bedroll.

Teeg dropped the note on Amanda's bedroll, then pushed Cloris ahead of him out the door to the wagon where Runt was waiting for them. He was about seventeen years old with a pockmarked face, blue eyes, and dirty blond hair that hung below his filthy hat.

"Ulrie, help the lady in," Teeg said with a gruff laugh as he mounted his horse.

Ulrie tossed in Cloris's bedroll and pack, then lifted her easily into the back of the wagon. The feel of his hands at her waist sent chills down her spine. She pulled away from him and sank to a tarp on the floor of the wagon. She wanted to shout for Amanda, but she kept her mouth closed. The men might kill her and Amanda too if she didn't cooperate.

All day long Cloris huddled in the back of the swaying, jostling wagon as Runt drove out into the prairie looking for meat. Teeg and Ulrie rode beside the wagon, often riding out of sight to hunt for antelope. At night they camped by a stream where she built a fire, broke through the ice for water, and roasted rabbits and baked cornbread. She didn't want to eat, but she was too hungry not to. Cold wind chilled her back even while her front side grew too hot from being close to the fire. The smell of smoke burned her nose. She felt the men watching her, but they kept their distance. She slept lightly, always on guard, then rose early to make breakfast.

Her days fell into the same routine—travel, cook, travel, cook, sleep. When Teeg wasn't around, Ulrie talked to her even though he wasn't supposed to. She tried to ignore him, but he persisted, and that frightened her. He was getting too friendly for her comfort.

They headed down into Nebraska, and her pulse raced. Could she find Carl White and stay with him? But if she did, what would become of Amanda?

One morning Cloris watched the men ride away from camp, taking Runt with them this time. They'd said today they'd butcher cattle if they came across them since they hadn't had any luck in finding antelope. Ulrie turned in the saddle and lifted his hat. Wind tangled his red hair, and he laughed. She trembled at the sight. If he came back alone, Teeg wouldn't be there to keep him in line. Maybe this was her chance to get away. Her stomach cramped just thinking about the danger. Teeg had said, "I'm leavin' you alone, Cloris. You ain't dumb enough to walk out into them sandhills and get lost, what with a storm headin' our way. That's a mighty painful death. And if we have to hunt you down, that'll be a worse death."

Frantically she looked around. If she headed southwest, maybe she'd find Jake's Crossing or even a ranch. Her hand trembling, she poured the rest of the coffee into a mug and gulped it down. It tasted bitter, but the hot drink warmed her slightly. She ate the last bite of cornbread but was still hungry. They'd kept her on the verge of hunger from the very first day. Teeg said she'd stick around as long as her belly touched her backbone.

She put out the campfire, then stood there in the great silence of the sandhills. Should she go or stay? She thought of the years she'd stayed with Aunt Prescott because she'd been too frightened to leave. "I won't let that happen again," she muttered grimly. She looked up into the gray sky. "Heavenly Father, You are always with me even when it doesn't feel like it. Help me again today. I need to find Carl White or somebody who'll help me get away from the hunters." She prayed on until finally she could move.

With determined steps she ran to the wagon and lifted out her bedroll and her pack. She spotted Runt's long leather coat and hat and put them on, thankful for the extra warmth. She didn't feel good about stealing but figured the men owed her something for taking her captive. She walked away from the wagon and away from the camp, out into the dried grass of the prairie. In every direction all she saw was rolling hills and wide valleys. She picked out a hill as her guide and walked toward it. When she reached that hill, she chose another, and then another, until she was far away from the campsite. The wind blew harder against her back, and the sky turned darker. She knew the storm was quickly getting closer. Would she freeze to death in a blizzard in the Nebraska sandhills? She shivered, then determinedly shook her head. She would make it to safety! There was no going back!

She trudged on with her head down. Often she stopped to listen for hoofbeats or a wagon, but all she heard was her heavy breathing and the sound of the powerful wind. Her lungs ached, and the bedroll grew almost too heavy to carry.

Just before dark she found shelter in a narrow valley between two short hills. She used her pack as a pillow, then curled up in her bedroll just as snow began to fall. Wind whipped the snow into a whirling, swirling mass. She covered her head and huddled close to the side of the hill. The smell of the leather coat turned her stomach at first, but she grew used to it. She dozed but was too cold to fall into a deep sleep.

Hours later she heard the wind die down. She tried to move but couldn't. Snow sifted down inside her blanket. With all her strength she lifted her hands and pushed the blanket up and back. She burst out of a layer of snow and looked all around at the miles of snowy hills. The sky was almost as white as the snow.

"Please, God, don't let me die out in this snowy wilderness!" she whispered hoarsely. Then she shouted it. The sound of her voice was loud in the stillness around her. Tears smarted in her eyes.

Slowly, carefully, she picked her way through the deep snow in the direction she was sure was south. Suddenly the wind started to blow again, sending the snow flying through the air as if it were still snowing. She found shelter out of the wind, covered herself with her bedroll, and waited. The waiting went on and on and on. Could she bear waiting another minute? "Help me!" she cried. "Help me!"

Just then she heard someone shout, "Are you lost?"

Cloris jumped up, and the blanket fell to the snowy ground. A girl on the back of a horse was right in front of her. The horse reared, and the girl fell to the ground. The horse galloped away.

Unable to move, Cloris stared at the girl in fright.

10 Caught!

Her eyes wide, Sadie leaned against the sand of the blowout where she and Cloris had taken shelter for the night near the Circle Y cattle. She shook her head in wonder as her new friend finished her story. "What an adventure! Did you know who I was when I found you?"

"No. You said your name was Sadie Merrill, but I finally figured out you were Sadie York."

"Do you still have Carl's letters?"

Cloris shook her head sadly. "They're at the camp in my pillow case. But Amanda will save them for me, I'm sure." Cloris trembled. "I have to find a way to help her! If the hunters go back without me, they might kill Amanda."

"Caleb will find a way to help you," Sadie said with more assurance than she felt. She'd never heard such a story as Cloris had told her, but she knew it was all true. She wanted to do something to help Cloris find Carl White and also to bring Amanda to live near them.

"When did you see Carl White last?" Cloris asked hesitantly.

"Sunday at church."

"In the little sod schoolhouse?"

Sadie laughed and nodded. It felt funny that a stranger knew so much about all of them.

"Did he say anything about his mail-order bride?"

Sadie shook her head. "He's not one to talk about private things. We heard he's been expecting a mail-order bride, but she never showed up."

Cloris pulled her knees to her chest and folded her arms on them. Wind blew snow across in front of her. A cow mooed, and then all was quiet. She wanted to ask dozens of questions, but she wasn't sure she should. "Was he sad about her not showing up?"

Sadie shrugged. "I reckon, but he didn't say."

"What'll he do when he learns I'm not Marlene?"

"Once you tell him what you told me, he'll be glad you came instead of Marlene. He's a real nice man."

Cloris sighed in relief. "I learned to love him because of his letters, but he doesn't know anything about me. It's frightening."

Sadie thought about Levi and the valentine she was making for him. Her problem was tiny compared to Cloris's.

They talked quietly long into the night, then drifted off to sleep with the comforting sounds of cattle nearby.

In the morning Sadie woke up with a start. What had awakened her? Trembling, she nudged

Cloris out of her sleep. "I heard something," Sadie whispered.

Cloris jumped up, leaving the blanket at her feet. Shivering with cold and fear, she looked around. The cattle were in the valley where they'd been last night. "I don't see or hear anything or anybody," she said softly just in case she was wrong. She didn't want her voice to carry on the wind.

"I must've been wrong." Sadie folded the blanket and placed it in Cloris's pack. "We have to find something to eat." If she had a gun, she could easily shoot a rabbit. She looked at the cattle. "A steak would be good."

"It would." Cloris looked longingly at the cattle. It had been a long time since she'd been comfortably full. She'd never gone hungry at Aunt Prescott's. Cloris frowned. She'd rather go hungry the rest of her life than return there!

"We'll stay with the cattle." Sadie pushed back her braids and settled her hat in place. "Riley and Caleb will find them . . . and us."

Just then Sadie spotted a movement on the far side of the herd. She nudged Cloris and pointed.

"It's Ulrie," Cloris whispered with a shiver.

Sadie gasped, then darted a look around for the other two. She didn't see them. She looked back at Ulrie just as he slit a cow's throat with the knife he always carried. Blood spurted, and the cow fell at his feet, its legs jerking convulsively. He turned to another animal and slit its throat, then another.

Cloris bit back a scream, then grabbed Sadie before she cried out. "Don't make a sound," Cloris hissed.

Numbly Sadie nodded. She watched in horror as Teeg joined Ulrie to gut and skin the cows. The wagon stopped near them, and Runt climbed down to help. The smell reached Sadie, and she gagged. If only she could have stopped the men from killing Caleb's cows! Each cow killed was cash money out of Caleb's hand.

Cloris led Sadie around the hill and out of sight of the men and the cattle. Wind blew the sounds and the smells to them. A weak sun peeked through the clouds but didn't bring any warmth nor much light.

"We have to stop them before they kill all of Caleb's cattle," Sadie said frantically.

"There's nothing we can do."

Tears streamed down Sadie's cheeks. She'd never felt so helpless in her whole life. Silently she asked the Lord to show her how she could stop the men from doing their evil deeds. There had to be a way.

Just then she heard the sound of a pistol being cocked right behind her. Fear pricked her skin.

"Hands up, ladies," Ulrie said with a chuckle.

Cloris gasped as she spun around to face the big redhead. Why hadn't she heard him?

Her hands over her head, Sadie faced the man squarely. She'd never let him know how much he frightened her!

Ulrie lowered his gun and grinned at Cloris. "You didn't stay put. But I see you got us another helper."

Sadie started to say Caleb would be there soon, but she saw Cloris shake her head just enough to let her know to keep the information to herself.

"What's your name, girl?" Ulrie asked.

"Sadie."

"Sadie, you and Cloris are gonna cook us dinner right now. We got some steaks cooling in the snow. There's cornmeal and flour in the wagon.

Some beans too. Get a move on, ladies. We're a hungry crew."

Cloris tried to relax but couldn't. Ulrie sounded just fine, but the hard look in his eyes said something different. Did he plan to keep them prisoners until they reached the gold camp, or would he shoot them before they got to Dakota Territory?

Sadie moved closer to Cloris as they walked around the herd of cattle to the camp the men had set up. Ashes lay in a heap where the fire had been. The blackened coffeepot sat in the snow nearby.

"We want to eat right away, so get to work." Ulrie waved his hand at them, then strode away. He stopped and looked over his shoulder. "Don't try to run away. I've got my eye on you both. I can shoot straight and fast, and I'll do it if I have to."

Cloris groaned. Freedom had been so short! She looked around for wood to start the fire, but there wasn't a tree or bush in sight. "How does he expect us to build a fire?"

"With dried cow manure." Sadie explained how they'd burned cow chips ever since they'd come to the Circle Y to live. She showed Cloris how to find the dry ones. "Don't touch the wet ones. They stink, and they're real messy."

"I can imagine," Cloris said, rolling her eyes.

Soon they had a fire blazing and a reserve pile of cow chips nearby. Cloris made the coffee with water from the barrel the hunters had brought, while Sadie mixed a batch of cornbread to bake in the cast-iron pot called a spider. She opened a can of beans and put them on to heat. The smell of the beans, the coffee, and the baking cornbread made her mouth water and her stomach knot. Would the smell drift across the sandhills to Caleb and Riley and show them where she was? Silently she prayed for them to come.

Cloris fried the steaks, sending out a mouth-watering aroma. She called the men, and they hurried to the camp, rubbing their hands with snow to clean off the blood.

Teeg eyed Sadie, scowled at Cloris, then filled his tin plate.

Seeming not to notice Cloris or Sadie, Runt filled his plate. He stuffed a bite of cornbread into his mouth before he hunkered down to eat in earnest.

"Looks mighty good." His plate full, Ulrie smiled at Cloris, then joined Teeg.

Sadie ate hungrily, and she noticed Cloris did too. They didn't talk until they'd eaten two thick steaks and a pile of beans along with coffee and cornbread. Sadie didn't like the taste of the coffee, but it was hot and wet and felt good inside her. She watched the men eat three steaks each along with another batch of cornbread, all the beans, and a whole pot of coffee. After they ate, Teeg and Ulrie sat there smoking and talking while Runt dropped off to sleep.

Several minutes later Teeg kicked Runt to wake him, then turned to Cloris. "You fix a supper that good too and we might not shoot you."

The color drained from her face. She pulled Sadie close to her side and watched the men walk back to the cattle to butcher more.

Sadie groaned at every cow that fell dead. Would Momma ever get the frame house she wanted?

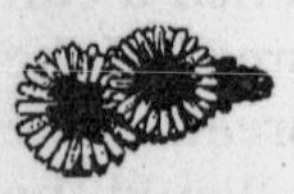

The Rescue

His heart heavy, Caleb rode beside Riley, heading toward home. They hadn't found all the cattle, and, worse, Sadie Rose was missing.

"Maybe she went home," Riley said for the tenth time since she'd turned up missing.

"I'd sure like to think so." Caleb couldn't stand the thought of little Sadie Rose lost in the prairie without a rifle. She was strong and bright, but the snowy sandhills were deceptive.

Caleb reined up and turned to Riley, who stopped beside him. "We can't go home yet, son. I got this gut feelin' that we should keep lookin'."

Riley grinned in relief. "Me too! I sure didn't want to go back yet."

"You should've told me."

"You're the boss." Riley still couldn't get used to being able to talk to Caleb man to man. When Pa was alive, Riley had to keep his thoughts to himself and his mouth shut unless Pa asked him a direct question. That's the way Pa wanted it.

"The Good Book says, 'A righteous man's steps are ordered of the Lord,'" Caleb said in his soft Texas drawl. "We're righteous because of Jesus, and He directs us one way or the other." Caleb lifted his eyes toward Heaven. "Father God, You know where Sadie Rose is. Direct our steps so we'll find her. Thank You."

"Thank You," Riley whispered. He liked the way Caleb trusted God for everything. Riley was learning to do the same.

Caleb urged Bay forward, then stopped. In his heart he knew he was going in the wrong direction. He turned Bay and urged him to go southwest instead.

Riley hunched down into his collar to try to keep warm as he followed Caleb. They'd eaten dinner about an hour ago, but Riley's stomach growled with hunger. He had food in his pack, but he knew he needed to ration it carefully. His canteen bumped against his leg. They were rationing their water too. Just the thought of not having all the water to drink that he wanted made him thirsty. He rolled saliva around in his mouth and swallowed it.

About an hour later Caleb reined in and motioned for Riley to keep quiet. "I smell smoke," Caleb said in a low, tight voice. "I'll ride up that hill and have a look-see. Keep your eyes peeled."

Riley nodded.

Caleb urged Bay forward up the hill. Before he reached the top, Caleb slipped out of the saddle and crept the rest of the way on foot. When he pulled off his wide-brimmed hat, icy wind ruffled his hair. He slowly stood and looked around. His pulse leaped.

He saw cattle with a wagon beside them. A campfire burned nearby, and two people stood beside it. He was too far away to make out who they were. Maybe Sadie Rose had found them and joined them. He narrowed his eyes and saw a cow fall over. His heart jerked. Someone was killing cattle! Was it possible they were Circle Y stock? He eased down and slid downhill to Bay, then rode back to Riley. Caleb quickly reported what he'd seen. "We'll ride as close as we can without showin' ourselves, then walk to the camp. We can't be too careful."

Riley touched the rifle in the boot of his saddle. He'd helped catch cattle rustlers before, and he knew what to do. With both excitement and fear rising inside him, he rode around the hill behind Caleb.

Several minutes later they dismounted and left their mounts behind. As long as the reins hung down, the horses stayed put. Caleb had trained them that way.

Rifle in hand, Riley followed Caleb toward a hill that separated them from the valley where the cattle were. Caleb's whip hung off his shoulder. He carried a Bowie knife in a sheath on his right hip and a wooden-handled Colt .45 on his left hip. From the valley a man shouted and another answered. The smell of butchered animals drifted on the wind.

Caleb stopped short, and Riley almost bumped into him. Carefully Caleb peered around the hill. He was close enough to the campfire to recognize Sadie Rose, but he didn't know the red-haired woman with her. His mouth turned bone-dry. Was Sadie Rose safe? He motioned to Riley to take a look.

Riley eased around the hill enough to see the camp and the cattle. He saw Sadie and wanted to call to her, but he forced back the shout.

Caleb narrowed his eyes to read the brand on

the cattle. The men were butchering *his* cattle! More importantly, Sadie Rose was in danger! How could he get her attention without alerting the men or the woman beside Sadie Rose? He looked down at the snow. Could he hit her with a snowball from this distance? He pulled back and whispered his plan to Riley.

"I can do it, Daddy," Riley whispered. He and Web had made up a game with snowballs. They'd made a circle with a bull's-eye on the side of the barn, then pitched snowballs at it. They added up points on who got the closest. He got so good at it, he could hit the bull's-eye every time.

Caleb agreed to let Riley do the throwing. "But don't hit the woman beside Sadie Rose."

"I won't." Riley handed Caleb the rifle, then packed a ball of snow in his hands. A shiver trickled down his spine. Could he really hit Sadie and not the woman? He drew back and threw the snowball. It fell short of Sadie, and she didn't notice it.

Riley flushed and glanced at Caleb.

"Try again," Caleb whispered. "You almost got her."

Riley packed another snowball. His hands were cold from the snow. He drew back, paused, then threw the snowball with all his might. It struck Sadie on the thigh.

Sadie jumped and yelped, then looked down at the circle of snow on her leg. Someone had hit her with a snowball! It couldn't have been the hunters. All three were busy butchering cattle. Her heart stood still. Had Caleb or Riley struck her to get her attention?

"Is something wrong?" Cloris whispered sharply.

Sadie shook her head. "I think my daddy and

brother are here." She looked in the direction from which the snowball had to have come. Nobody was in sight. As she looked, she caught sight of a hat—Caleb's hat. She sucked in air. Slowly she lifted her hand to let them know she knew they were there. How could she help them?

Behind the hill Caleb whispered in relief, "She saw us. Now we have to catch those men without spooking the cattle."

Riley frowned as he looked at the open space between them and the herd.

"We'll come up on them from the other side of the hill and get the drop on 'em." Caleb motioned to the hill as he related the plan. Then they ran along the base of the hill so they could come out on the far side.

At the campfire Sadie stood very still and waited for something to happen. What were Caleb and Riley planning?

"Let's get out of here while the men are too busy to notice," Cloris whispered, tugging on Sadie's arm.

Sadie nodded. Her insides quivering, Sadie walked to the hill with Cloris close beside her. They ducked around it, expecting to see Caleb and Riley. But they weren't there.

"Where are they?" Cloris asked in alarm.

"Probably going around the hill that way." Sadie saw footprints in the snow that led away from the hill. She knew their horses would be waiting there. "I'll get their horses." She ran in the footprints, excitement building inside her. Soon they'd be on their way home with the cattle and with Cloris safe with them.

Cloris hesitated, then ran after Sadie. They found the horses and led them toward the camp.

Riley peeked around the hill. The wagon was

closer than he'd thought. He motioned to Caleb that he was going to make a dash for the wagon.

"Be careful," Caleb mouthed.

Riley nodded, then sprinted to the back of the wagon. The men were bent over a cow and hard at work. They didn't even notice him. The smell of guts and hides turned Riley's stomach. His mouth filled with bile, but he swallowed hard and willed his stomach to settle. Steam rose from the piles of innards lying in the blood-soaked snow. The hides were tossed into the back of the wagon.

Caleb waited until Riley was in place, then stepped out in plain sight. His whip in his hand, he walked toward the hunters. He stopped several feet from them and said in a solemn, calm voice, "Drop the knives, boys, and reach for the sky."

Riley stepped into sight then too, his rifle aimed at Ulrie who was nearest to him. "Don't go for your guns. You don't stand a chance."

The men dropped their knives and slowly stood, their arms held high.

Teeg eyed Caleb. "There's plenty of beef for all of us. Tell the kid to put down the gun so we can talk."

"They got my brand on 'em, boys. You're butchering cattle that don't belong to you." Caleb's voice was deceptively gentle.

"We thought they were strays," Ulrie said with a forced laugh.

"We was hired to take meat to the goldfields in Dakota Territory." Teeg slowly lowered his hands. "There's good money in it. Enough for you, too."

"You got it wrong, cowboy," Ulrie said. "We paid for these cattle. I got a bill of sale right in my pocket." He reached for it.

"Don't try it!" Caleb sent the whip snaking through the air. It caught Ulrie's wrist as he pulled out a small gun. The gun flew from the man's grasp, and he swore in pain.

Caleb flicked the whip and slowly coiled it as he walked closer to the men. "Get over by the campfire . . . now!" The command cracked almost as loudly as his whip had. Just then he saw Sadie lead the horses into sight. "Tie 'em up, Sadie Rose," he called to her.

She laughed and nodded. "Want to help, Cloris?"

"I certainly do!" Cloris lifted the coiled rope off the saddle horn and quickly tied Runt and Teeg together.

Sadie dropped a loop around Ulrie and tied him so he couldn't get away. She looped the end of the rope around the saddle horn. If Ulrie tried to get away, Bay would pull the rope tight. "Tie your rope this same way, Cloris."

Cloris did, then stepped back. She watched as Teeg and Runt tried to step close to the horse in order to loosen the loops around them. The horse backed away, keeping the rope taut. Finally the men gave up and dropped in a heap on the ground.

With a happy shout Sadie ran to Caleb and flung her arms around him.

He held her tight. "Thank God you're safe!"

"I prayed you'd find us." Sadie turned to Riley and hugged him too. He flushed, but she just hugged him tighter.

"You always get yourself in a fix, don't you, Sadie?" Riley chuckled as he stepped away from her.

"Not always." Sadie laughed as she motioned to Cloris. "I want you to meet my friend Cloris." Sadie introduced them, then stood back and listened as Cloris explained how she'd come to be with the hunters. She didn't tell them about being Carl White's mail-order bride.

Cloris took a deep breath. "I know this is asking a lot, but could you help me get my friend Amanda?"

Caleb rubbed a hand across his face.

"Please, Daddy!" Sadie slipped her hand into Caleb's. "I said you would."

Caleb chuckled. "Then how can I say no? We'll take the cattle home, turn these men over to Joshua Cass, then head north."

"The miners will pay you for the beef," Cloris said.

"I'll give it some thought. I don't reckon we can use that much meat." Caleb looked at the pile of slaughtered cattle and groaned. Maybe he could get cash money to put away for the frame house. "Riley, let's finish these last two cows and load 'em in the wagon."

Several minutes later Sadie stood alone with Cloris. "Why didn't you tell them about Carl?"

"I was too embarrassed," Cloris whispered.

"Don't be! They'd understand, just like I did. Carl might want to help get Amanda."

Cloris's stomach fluttered. "It would be wonderful if he did." Maybe she'd see Carl White soon. But what would she say to him?

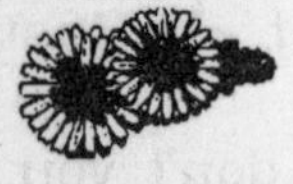

12 Carl White

Sadie squeezed Cloris's arm. "Don't be afraid. Tell Carl just what you told me. He'll understand."

Cloris nodded hesitantly, her mouth too dry to speak. She looked helplessly at Caleb in the wagon, where he was waiting to take her to see Carl, then on up to the gold camp to sell the frozen beef and get Amanda. Cloris bit her lip. Could she go with him? She had to! This was not the time to allow her fear to hold her back. As long as she could remember, she'd not taken action because she was afraid of something or someone. Not this time!

She hugged Sadie one last time, waved to the York family standing nearby, then climbed up beside Caleb. The sun shone brightly in the wide, blue sky.

"Relax, Cloris," Caleb said as he flicked the reins. "God is with you!"

"I know," she whispered. She braced her feet to

keep from falling off the high seat of the wagon as it swayed and bucked out onto the prairie.

Close to an hour later Caleb stopped outside a small sod house. Smoke curled out of the chimney. A horse nickered in the corral. "I'll drive over to visit Sven and Kara while you talk with Carl." Caleb motioned to the sod house off in the distance.

Just then the door opened, and Carl White stepped out, filling the doorway. He stood well over six feet tall and weighed over two hundred pounds. He held his wide-brimmed white hat in his hands. The wind ruffled his dark hair. He smiled at Caleb and looked questioningly at the redheaded woman he'd never seen before.

Cloris couldn't breathe as she studied him from head to toe. Carl White was standing before her in the flesh! Her dream had finally come true!

Caleb tipped his hat. "Morning, Carl. I brought you a visitor. She'll tell you who she is and why she's here. I'll head over to Sven's while you two talk."

Cloris trembled as she started to climb from the wagon. Could she really tell him the truth?

Dropping his hat on his head, Carl jumped forward and reached for Cloris. His hands closed around her waist, and she felt the jolt deep in her heart. He lowered her to the ground, then stepped quickly away from her.

Caleb slapped the reins on the team and drove slowly away. The sound of the rattling harness and creaking wagon hung in the air between Cloris and Carl.

"We'd best go inside where it's warmer," Carl finally said. He felt awkward being alone with the stranger. He thought of the pile of dirty dishes on the table and the unmade bed. Why hadn't he cleaned up a bit after chores this morning?

Cloris felt his hesitation, and fear kept her rooted to the spot. Her eyes glistened with tears. "I know I'm a bother coming here this way," she said hoarsely.

He saw her tears and the frightened look on her face, and he suddenly wanted to made her feel relaxed and comfortable with him. He smiled and took her arm. "You're no bother at all. Come right in! I have a little coffee left." He laughed and shook his head. "And the place is a mess."

Cloris relaxed enough to walk inside with him. The house was dark after the bright sunlight. Lamplight glowed across the table and onto the dirty dishes and Carl's Bible that he'd been reading. Sunlight filtered weakly through the dirty window near the unmade bed. It was a small house, but not nearly as small as the shack she'd lived in the past five months. And there was heat—blessed heat! For five months she'd been constantly cold. She wouldn't be cold in Carl's house.

"Let me take your coat." Carl took it from her, then wondered where to lay it—across the unmade bed, over a chair, or beside his coat on the peg by the door. Finally he hung it over his. Seeing a woman's coat there made him think of Marlene. His heart turned over, and a sick feeling filled his stomach. Why hadn't she come when she said she would? Had she backed out because she'd decided she couldn't be a mail-order bride? Or maybe she'd realized she didn't really care for him.

Taking off her bonnet, Cloris sank weakly to a chair. There were only two chairs in the whole place. Wood snapped in the small cast-iron cookstove, and she jumped, then laughed self-consciously. "I'm nervous—as you can probably tell."

"No need to be." He took the bonnet and hung

it with her coat. Feeling large and awkward in the tiny space, he turned to face her. Her red hair was a bright flame in the room. He'd always liked red hair. He pushed the thought abruptly aside. "York said you had something to tell me."

"You'd better sit down first," she said weakly.

He sat down, suddenly feeling weak in the knees. He closed his Bible and set it aside. Why hadn't he washed the dishes this morning? He picked up the pile and carried them to the shelf where he'd stack them when they were clean. He'd wash them later. "I'm sorry the place is dirty."

"It's all right, Carl, honestly it is."

Her speaking his name sent a funny feeling through him. He sat down again, his eyes on her, his nerves tight. "You know my name, but I don't know yours."

She swallowed hard. She could say she was Marlene Vines and never have to explain anything, but she couldn't lie—not to Carl White, a man of integrity. "I'm Cloris Rupert." She hesitated. "From Boston, Massachusetts."

"Boston? Do you know . . . Marlene Vines?" It hurt to speak her name aloud.

Cloris barely nodded.

Carl sank back weakly in his chair. "Is she . . . coming here?"

"No," Cloris whispered.

The color drained from Carl's face. For a minute he couldn't speak. "Why are you here?"

"I'm her cousin." As carefully and kindly as she could, Cloris told Carl about herself, about Marlene, and about the wonderful letters he'd written. At the end of the story she said, "I've come in Marlene's place."

"You? But I don't even know you!"

"You didn't know Marlene either or you couldn't have loved her."

"How do I know your story is true? Marlene might be kind and considerate and helpful. You might be the selfish one."

"But I'm not."

Carl wanted to jump up and pace the room, but there wasn't enough space. "What do you want of me?"

Cloris trembled and almost lost her nerve, but forced herself to speak. "I want us to get to know each other. I want to be your mail-order bride." The last words came out in a mere whisper and took every ounce of courage she had.

Reeling from what she'd said, Carl shook his head. "I love Marlene. How can I marry you?"

"You love what Marlene said about herself." Cloris took a deep breath and plunged on. "Just as I love what you said about yourself."

He flushed. "I'm not ready to hear that."

"I'm sorry." She watched the lamp flicker and smelled the kerosene. "I know you're not, but I wanted you to know—to understand."

He stabbed his fingers through his dark hair and rubbed his hand over his jaw. "You make me feel obligated to marry you."

Cloris looked at him in alarm. "No! Never that! I want us to get acquainted. If you don't want to marry me, I'll go away." She didn't know where, but she'd find somewhere to go. Pain ripped through her at the terrible thought. She wanted to be here with Carl.

"I'll give it some thought." Slowly he stood. He handed her her bonnet and coat, then slipped his on. He blew out the lamp. "York's waited long enough."

Cloris fumbled with the the string on her bonnet. "Are you going with us to get Amanda?"

Carl nodded.

Cloris smiled. "Thank you."

Her smile touched his heart, and he turned abruptly away and opened the door. He wasn't ready to open his heart to this stranger, but the least he could do was help get her friend.

Cloris stepped outdoors, blinking against the bright sunlight. She looked around and smiled. Would she live here soon? She glanced at Carl, and the smile died. Her heart heavy, she fell into step beside Carl as they walked toward Sven's place.

Amanda

Shivering with cold and hunger and frustration, Amanda sank weakly to a chair in the diner and leaned her elbows on the table. Where were Cloris and the hunters? Had they killed Cloris? Tears glistened in Amanda's eyes. "I should've stayed in New York!"

Cloris stepped inside and heard Amanda. "No! You're going with me!"

Amanda jumped up with a squeal. "Cloris! I thought something terrible happened to you!"

"It did, but I'm all right now." Cloris hugged Amanda, then stepped back and introduced her to Carl White and Caleb York.

Carl tipped his hat and smiled. It looked to him like Amanda was about to collapse. How could she survive in such a miserable place?

"Any friend of Cloris's is a friend of mine," Caleb

said with his hat in his hand. He'd heard how bad the gold camps were, but this was worse than he'd thought. He wanted to take the women away before another miserable minute passed.

Looking quickly from Carl to Cloris, Amanda wanted to ask about them but didn't. She knew Cloris would tell her in due time. She pulled her coat tightly about her and tried to stop shivering.

"We brought beef." Cloris quickly explained about the cattle. "Caleb is asking a fair price for it."

"I sold the business to Ernie from New Jersey." Amanda hurried to the door and shouted, "Ernie, get in here. You've got beef! You're in business!"

Cloris smiled proudly at Amanda. "Good for you for selling! Does that mean you're going with me?"

Amanda bit her lip. She glanced at the men, then back at Cloris. "I figured I'd go back home. To my old job."

"No! You can't!"

"It's security at least. And it's warm there. I'm so tired of being cold and hungry!"

Cloris wrapped an arm around Amanda. "I know . . . I know . . . But come with me . . . We'll find a warm place, and we won't go hungry." Could she say that for sure? A shiver trickled down her spine.

Ernie walked in and shouted, "What's this about beef?" He was a short, wide man with salt-and-pepper hair and a wool coat that looked two sizes too large on him. He'd told Amanda he won it in a poker game.

Amanda introduced Ernie all around, then said, "Talk to this man about prices."

"Let's go look at it first," Caleb said. He led the way outdoors to the wagon, with Ernie and Carl following.

Inside the diner Amanda excitedly caught

Cloris's hands. "I've got to know! What about you and Carl?"

Cloris swallowed hard and looked ready to cry. "He took it hard—about Marlene. We talked on the way here, and he likes me well enough. Just not enough to marry me."

"Oh, Cloris! What'll you do?"

"Caleb said we could stay with them. They have a small sod house where a woman named Adabelle Hepford is staying. We can share the house with her."

"Then what? How will we live? What will we do?"

"I don't know, but God will provide. I know that."

Amanda slowly nodded. "You're right. He will provide, just like He always has. He sent Ernie here to buy this place when I was ready to walk out in the prairie and just keep walking. And He sent you to be my friend, the first friend I've ever had in my life."

Cloris brushed tears from her eyes. She'd had two friends in her life—Bernice and Amanda. And after meeting the York family she knew she'd have a whole lot more. It would be the same with Amanda.

Several minutes later Cloris looked around the shack they'd lived in for the past five months. "How'd we ever survive in this tiny pile of boards?"

"We did what we had to do," Amanda said quietly as she gathered up her pack and her bedroll.

Cloris hugged the pillow with Carl's letters inside. She'd never give them up, no matter what Carl decided.

Outdoors the men scrubbed down the wagon, then spread clean straw in the bed. Caleb had sold the meat and the hides to Ernie. Ernie said he'd tan the hides and sell them for a profit. Caleb touched the roll of money in his pocket and smiled. He wouldn't have to disappoint Bess. She'd get her frame house in the spring. By her birthday, May 11, he'd have the house done. He turned to Carl with a grin. "A wife's a good thing, my friend."

Carl scowled. "The right wife. How do I know Cloris is telling the truth?"

"Your heart knows." Caleb clamped his hand on Carl's shoulder. "Remember, 'the steps of a righteous man are ordered of the Lord.' You'll know the right step to take with Cloris."

"Thank you." Carl looked toward the small shack where Cloris and Amanda were. It was too short for him to stand upright in. "That's no place for ladies."

"You're plumb right about that. I'm glad they're going with us. Adabelle says they can stay with her."

"Good." Carl felt some of the pressure vanish. He would have time to pray about Cloris as well as to get to know her. If what she'd told him was true, she was one exceptional lady.

Caleb filled the water barrel and loaded the box of food Ernie gave him for the trip back, while Carl tucked a bundle of wood under the seat. They'd camp tonight and get home tomorrow. Caleb studied the clouds and the sky. It didn't look like bad weather was coming.

Later Cloris and Amanda sat in the back of the wagon and watched the gold camp fade from sight. They looked at each other and laughed. They were free again!

Carl glanced back at them from where he sat beside Caleb. He wondered what they were laughing about. He wanted to laugh with them. He turned back and watched the hills in front of him, straining to hear what the women said. But he couldn't hear them over the creak of the wagon. He wanted to climb back and join them, but he didn't have the courage.

That night Cloris huddled in her bedroll and listened to the crack of the fire. She and Amanda had fixed a good meal from the supplies Ernie had sent with them, they'd talked a while, and then they all turned in. Cloris knew from Amanda's deep breathing that she was already asleep. It was probably the first night she'd let herself sleep soundly in a very long time. Stars twinkled high above in the night sky. A wolf howled, and the team of horses nickered nervously. They were hobbled to keep them from running away in the night.

On the other side of the campfire Carl lay wide awake, with York sleeping soundly beside him. Carl looked through the flames that were the color of Cloris's hair. Was she already asleep? He'd talked to her a little at supper, but she didn't push herself on him. That pleased him. He'd been afraid she'd cling to him like a sandburr and not give him a chance to think or breathe. What if she decided she wasn't really interested in him now that they'd met face to face and talked? His nerves tightened. He didn't want that to happen. But why? He couldn't answer his own question. Finally he closed his eyes. Just as he was drifting off to sleep, he heard Cloris sobbing.

He jumped up and ran around to her. She was crying in her sleep! He hunkered down beside her and gently shook her by the shoulder.

She awakened with a jolt. Her face was wet with tears, and she brushed them away as she sat up. "What's wrong?" she whispered.

"You were crying," he said softly.

Then she remembered her dream, and she shivered. "I had a nightmare."

"It must've been a bad one."

"It was."

"Can you tell me about it?"

She shuddered. "I dreamed Marlene took your letters from me and locked me in Westland Insane Asylum. She wouldn't let me out." Cloris hugged the pillow case of letters to her. "And she made me watch while she burned your letters."

Carl's heart jerked strangely. "It was only a dream. You're all right now."

She smiled into his eyes. "I am. Thank you."

He touched her hand, smiled, then walked around the campfire to his bedroll. She was hugging his letters as if they were her life! Marlene hadn't even wanted them. He looked through the flames at Cloris. Would she make him a good wife?

She settled down in her bedroll and held the pillow of letters tightly against her heart. "Good night, Carl," she said softly.

"Good night, Cloris." Her name sounded good on his tongue, and he said it again. He closed his eyes and drifted off to sleep.

Cloris smiled, then sank into sleep again.

14

The Valentine Party

With her heart racing, Sadie stood near the front of the school and looked at the laughing, talking crowd. She was trying to find Levi. Heat radiated out of the potbellied stove. The smell of food combined with wet wool filled the room.

Sadie held Levi's valentine in her hand. It had lace around the edges and red cloth hearts glued on it.

Would he give her one? If he didn't, maybe she shouldn't give him the special one that had the word "LOVE" on it. Instead, she'd give him the second one she'd made for him that said "FRIEND" and had only one heart and no lace. It was hard to know what to do. She spotted Opal with El Hepford. Opal never had a problem telling El how she felt about him.

Across the room Sadie's mother, Bess, introduced Amanda and Cloris to the teacher, Flynn Greer.

"I'm pleased to meet you," Amanda said. Her heart skipped a beat as she smiled into Flynn's bright blue eyes. He had curly dark hair and wore a flowered vest under his suit coat. She was glad Adabelle had loaned her a dress to wear for the party. It was dark green and fit her narrow waist and flared out down to her ankles. She'd never owned such a nice dress.

"Welcome to our community," Flynn said. He dragged his eyes off Amanda to greet Cloris.

Near the door Carl White watched Cloris and Flynn talking. Jealousy shot through Carl, surprising him. Flynn was a smooth talker and could turn any woman's head.

Chuckling, Sven nudged Carl. "You'd better get over there and stake your claim before you lose her."

Carl scowled at Sven. "Mind your own business."

"You are my business. We were bachelors together, and now we can be happily married men together."

Kara slipped her hand through Carl's arm. "I like her, Carl. I'd like her as my neighbor and friend."

A muscle jumped in Carl's jaw. "Don't push me," he whispered sharply.

They laughed and walked away to talk to Adabelle Hepford and Judge Loggia, who would get married in early spring.

Just then Cloris looked across the room, and her eyes locked with Carl's. She smiled, and her heart flip-flopped. She'd made him a valentine. Would she have the courage to give it to him?

At the front of the room Sadie searched the noisy crowd for her best friend Mary. She was talking to Mitch Hepford. Sadie sighed heavily. It was hard to share Mary with Mitch.

Soon Flynn started the festivities by calling the Hepfords, Caleb York, and Judge Loggia to the front. Judge led them in prayer, then started singing "Marching to Zion." The walls seemed to bulge with the sound of the instruments and Judge's beautiful voice.

Sadie joined in the singing, her heart soaring with praise to God. She felt a movement beside her, and she turned her head. Levi Cass stood at her side. They smiled at each other, and Sadie sang even more loudly.

Cloris stood beside Amanda, and they joined in with the singing, both drinking in the glorious sound. They'd never heard such singing or felt such joy. This was a community to which they'd love to belong.

Carl tried to enjoy the singing but couldn't. He wished his pride hadn't kept him from standing with Cloris. She looked pretty in the blue dress with white collar and cuffs.

After the third song Caleb stepped forward with his guitar in his hand. He waited until everyone was quiet. "We want all of you to welcome two new women. We've introduced most of you to them, I reckon, but those we haven't, be sure to introduce yourselves. Cloris, Amanda, please come forward so everybody can get a good look at you."

Cloris flushed and hung back a little, but Amanda strode forward with her head high and her brown eyes shining as everyone clapped and cheered.

When everyone was quiet again Caleb said, "We're happy to have these two stayin' with us for the time bein'. I'm sure they'd like for you to call on them and get acquainted."

"We certainly would," Amanda said. Everyone laughed.

Cloris smiled. "It's a pleasure to be a part of this group. If we can be of help to any of you, let us know."

"I need a wife who can cook," Zane Hepford said with a hearty laugh and a quick pick on his banjo.

Everyone laughed again—except Carl. He hadn't thought of Zane Hepford as competition. Zane was too old for Cloris. He had a married son already. Carl could tell by the look on Zane's face that age wasn't going to matter. Carl wanted to shout that Cloris wasn't in the market for a husband, but he didn't have the nerve. He'd make sure he sat with her to eat. He wished he had a valentine for her. But maybe she wouldn't want it after the way he'd acted toward her.

Later Sadie found a quiet spot where she could talk to Levi. Her cheeks burned, and it was hard to speak. "I made you a valentine."

"I made you one too," he said, smiling.

"You did?" It was hard to breathe. "Will you give me mine first?"

Levi turned red. "Can't we do it at the same time?"

The valentines in her hand suddenly felt as heavy as a sack of grain. Which one should she give him? Mustering every bit of her courage, she decided to give him the lacy one with "LOVE" on it. She held it out to him as he held one out to her.

He took hers and read it, then smiled happily.

She read his, and her heart soared. He'd printed "ALWAYS BE MY VALENTINE. I LOVE YOU. LEVI." "Thank you," she whispered. Then she giggled. "I made another one for you in case I didn't have the courage to give you that one. Want it?"

"Sure." He chuckled. "I made two for you, but I left the other one home." He read the second one and laughed out loud. "That's just what *I* wrote! I'm glad we gave each other the ones we did."

Sadie whispered, "Me too." She took a deep, steadying breath. "I thought you'd be embarrassed."

"And I thought you'd slap my face." Levi squeezed her hand, then let it go before anyone saw. "Let's get in line to eat."

"Okay. I'm starved!" With her head held high, Sadie walked to the line with Levi.

A few feet away Carl felt rooted to the spot in the hard-packed dirt floor. He'd tried to get to Cloris to ask her to eat with him, but Zane Hepford had beat him to it. She was laughing at something Zane said. Carl looked longingly at the door. He needed fresh air. Finally he pried himself loose and slipped through the crowd and made his way to the door. He stepped outside and breathed deeply of the cold, fresh air. Stars twinkled above the prairie. Horses moved restlessly in the rope corral.

Carl walked away from the schoolhouse and stood alone with his hat in his hand. Loneliness swept over him. Would his pride keep him lonely forever?

Inside the schoolhouse Cloris had seen Carl go outdoors. She excused herself to Zane and followed as quickly as she could. She slipped on her cape and stepped out into the cold night. She spotted Carl a few feet away with his back to her. "Carl . . ." she said softly.

He hesitated, then turned. He was surprised to see her there. "I suppose you're going to eat with Zane."

"I declined his invitation. I said I was eating with you." She bit her lower lip as she slowly walked over to him. "Am I?"

He stared at her as if he hadn't heard right. "Is that what you want?"

She nodded. Slowly she held the valentine out to him. "I made it special for you before I left Boston. I know it's very presumptuous."

"Thank you." He looked at the lace and the hearts. "It's too dark to read it."

"Save it for when you're home tonight."

"I will." He pushed it into his pocket, and it felt warm against him.

Cloris locked her hands together as she looked up at Carl. "Today's my birthday."

"It is? I didn't know."

"I promised myself I'd have this birthday with you, Carl. I'm glad it happened." Before she lost her nerve, she stood on tiptoe and kissed the corner of his mouth. "I promised I'd do that too," she whispered breathlessly.

His heart thumped so hard, he was sure she heard it. "Do you go around kissing all the guys?"

"No. You're the only one . . . ever."

All his suspicions melted away. He took her face between his large hands and kissed her lips with a long, lingering kiss.

"Happy birthday, Cloris."

"Thank you!" She wanted to fling her arms around him, but she knew she ought to bide her time.

"Shall we go inside to eat together?"

"I'd like that."

He took her arm, and they walked back into the crowded sod schoolhouse. He saw the looks others gave them, but he only smiled. Let them look and talk all they wanted. Cloris was at his side, and that's what was important.

At the table heavy with food Sadie dished scalloped potatoes onto Levi's plate. "I made them," she said.

"They're my favorite."

"I know." Sadie grinned as they walked across the room to sit with Mary and Mitch.

Sadie glanced around the crowded school at her friends and family, and her heart swelled with pride. Nobody in the world could be as happy as she was right this minute in the little sod schoolhouse with the potbellied stove blazing hot with cow chips she'd help gather.

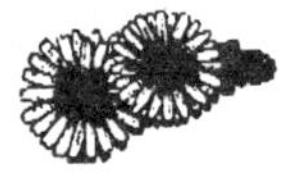